Medusa aimed her poisoned
arrow right at Lillian...

Lillian always loved stories about
myths and monsters—until she
found herself inside one, searching
for her lost sister.

Joined by her best friends, Katy
and Maisy, Lillian must cross a sea
guarded by krakens and sirens, race
through a dark forest haunted by
elves and chimeras, and pass through
mountains ruled by griffins and rocs.

Where in this world is Lillian's
sister? Who is the mysterious boy
with the stone medallion? Why
do the monsters hold an ancient
grudge against humanity? And
what is the secret hiding at the
heart of it all?

The
World
of
LANODEKA

THE MONSTER REALM. Copyright © 2014 by Nara Duffie.

Cover art, Lanodeka map and chapter illustrations by Elisabeth Alba. http://www.albaillustration.com

Author photo by Michael Negrete. http://michaelnegrete.com

ISBN 978-0-9849346-5-2

To Andrea

Thank you!

THE MONSTER REALM

A NOVEL BY

Nara Duffie

with Illustrations by Elisabeth Alba

roam
&ramble

To Ray Harryhausen

CONTENTS

The World of LANODEKA

MAP BY ELISABETH ALBA

THE MONSTER REALM

Prologue: A Girl Disappears

Spring Town was a small town. It was named Spring Town because it felt like spring all through the year, cool and sunny and green, then in December it turned cold and rainy and felt like winter.

On every street, leafy trees stood in a line. The branches grew into each other like a canopy, until winter came. Then the empty branches looked tangled and creepy, almost like skeletons.

On a March afternoon, Lillian sat in her room reading *Harry Potter and the Prisoner of Azkaban*. She was ten years old and tall for her age, healthy and strong. She had hazel-green eyes and light brown skin, and her wavy red hair fell to her shoulders. Lillian never wore makeup, not even to church or on birthdays.

Lillian loved mythology and monsters, especially Ray Harryhausen movies. She loved how his stop motion animation made the monsters look mythical instead of real. Ray's monsters were scary without being too scary.

Bluebell, Lillian's older sister, walked through the door. "Are you reading that book *again?*" she teased. "You must have read it a million times."

Lillian put down her book. She was reading the most exciting chapter, the most thrilling part of the whole novel. Then Bluebell strutted in, and Lillian was pulled out of the magical story.

If Lillian even peeked into her sister's room, Bluebell would yell at her to get out. If her mom and dad were around, Bluebell would yell at Lillian later. But she never forgot to yell at Lillian, and she never said she was sorry.

Bluebell wore a royal blue swimsuit and carried a big beach bag. She was sixteen, had dark green eyes and short, curly red hair. She never wore her hair up; she never even wore it in a hair band. She used a lot of dark blue eyeshadow and pale pink lipstick. She was impatient with everyone, especially with Lillian.

"I'm going to a beach party and sleepover, Lillian, and you're not invited," Bluebell smirked. "You'll have to stay home, and let me guess, when I'm gone you're going to watch *Clash of the Titans* for the millionth time, the most boring movie in the world. If by some slim chance you decide to watch something else, it'll probably be another Harryhausen movie or a Medusa documentary, if there is such a thing."

Lillian felt mad because she *was* going to watch *Clash of the Titans*. "It's not boring, unless you're talking about the remake."

"Lillian," said Bluebell as she walked out of the room, "they're *all* boring."

Lillian moved to her window. She watched Bluebell turn the corner and strut out of sight. She wished she could go too.

Lillian sat on her bed. Bluebell had lots of friends and got invited to lots of parties, though Lillian couldn't understand why. *She treats her friends worse than she treats me.*

Lillian had only two close friends and hardly got invited anywhere. She felt like she always had to stay home. No one wanted her around.

Only one thing would cheer her up. She popped *Clash of the Titans* into her DVD player. She knew that Perseus and Medusa, Andromeda and the Kraken, would make her feel better.

But by the end of the movie, she was still sad.

The next morning, the family waited for Bluebell to come home. When Bluebell didn't show up, her parents called Bluebell's friends who said there had been no beach party and no sleepover.

Lillian waited all afternoon. Her parents called the

police but they couldn't find Bluebell. No one found Bluebell. Days turned into weeks, and weeks into months. It was as if she had disappeared off the face of the earth.

Part One

THE MEDALLION

Chapter 1. Leaving Home

Beep beep beep! Beep beep beep!

Lillian woke with a start like she always did when her alarm clock went off. It was a bright spring day and the birds sang their morning songs.

Two years had passed since her sister disappeared. Lillian was twelve now, and her wavy red hair had grown almost to her waist. She looked out the window every morning, hoping to see Bluebell walking up the street. But she only saw empty sidewalks.

Lillian stood on her bed, opened her window, and stepped out onto the gable roof. She climbed into the mulberry tree near the house.

It was Bluebell's birthday today. Lillian carried a round wooden box, painted red. She pulled off the lid, reached inside and carefully took out a China doll. With a blue string, she tied the doll to a V-shaped branch. Headphones were tied higher up in the tree; there was also a makeup kit and some yarn for a scarf that Bluebell had wanted to knit. This was the place Lillian chose to put all of Bluebell's birthday gifts. The older gifts looked weathered and faded.

Katy and Maisy, Lillian's best friends, would come later to tie their gifts in the tree and eat mulberries.

Lillian went inside for one last thing: a nest she had found. It was a big owl's nest. She climbed back into the tree and put the nest in a tangle of branches. It was a good gift, because Bluebell had loved wild things. Lillian hoped that an owl would use it.

Lillian got dressed and went downstairs. Her dad sat at the kitchen table reading a book on the Kindle, and her mom was cooking hash browns for breakfast.

Her mom had green eyes and red, wavy hair down to her shoulders. She wore a plain red skirt with a green short-sleeved top. She waved the spatula. "Good morning, sweetheart."

Lillian waved to her mom and sat at the table. "Hi, dad." Her dad was too into his book to answer.

"Can I go to the beach?" Lillian asked. "I want to look for Bluebell again."

Her mom dropped the spatula. Her dad looked up from his book.

"Why do you want to go *now?*" he asked. He had

short brown hair and brown eyes. "You haven't been to the beach in two years."

"I have this strong feeling I can find her," said Lillian. "It's like I can almost hear Bluebell calling to me. I don't know how to explain it."

Her mom and dad exchanged a worried glance.

"What?" said Lillian.

"I really don't think it's a good idea," said her mom.

Lillian didn't argue. She decided to wait until Katy and Maisy came. Maybe they would understand.

Ding-dong, ding-dong!

Lillian rushed to the door. Katy and Maisy stood outside. They each held a little box.

The three girls went upstairs to Lillian's room. Maisy opened her box first. Inside, a western fence lizard crawled in jumpy circles.

"Remember how much she loved lizards?" said Maisy, taking the lizard out of the box.

"He's so cute," said Katy, reaching for the lizard.

"Back off, animal lover," said Maisy. She climbed through the window and released the lizard in the tree.

"That's perfect," said Lillian. "Thanks, Maisy."

Then Katy opened her gift. Inside the box was an expensive compass. "She loved to hike by herself. It's waterproof and shockproof."

"She would have loved this," said Lillian.

Katy handed the gift to Lillian, who climbed outside and hung the compass in the tree. Katy hated getting dirty. She wore her white-blond hair down to her waist, used a lot of makeup, and preferred clothes from the most popular brands.

"You always dress like you're going to a party," Maisy told Katy.

Maisy never wore makeup. She liked to get dirty, and cut her yellow, wavy hair to different lengths.

Lillian turned to Maisy and Katy. "You know how I've been having these feelings about Bluebell? It's like some kind of energy or intuition or something."

"Is it contagious?" asked Maisy.

"Maisy," said Katy. "This is serious."

"The feeling keeps getting stronger," said Lillian. "It's like someone's calling me. Sometimes I can't even sleep at night. I have to do something."

"Like see a doctor?" asked Maisy.

Katy gave Maisy a warning look, then turned to Lillian. "What do you want to do?"

Lillian paused and looked from Katy to Maisy. "I want to go find Bluebell."

Katy's face softened. "How? The police searched for two years. What can *we* do? Where would we even start?"

"How about the beach?" shrugged Maisy. "That's where she disappeared."

"I was thinking the same thing," said Lillian. "We can go tonight. We'll search the beach and see if there's anything to these feelings I've been having."

"My parents won't let me go to the beach at night," said Katy.

"That's why you don't tell them," said Maisy.

"We'll be back in the morning," promised Lillian, "before anyone knows we're gone."

"I'm in," said Maisy.

Katy looked worried. "I don't know ..."

Lillian leaned forward. "I need your help."

"Two against one," said Maisy.

Katy thought about how much Lillian meant to her, and of all the times Lillian had stood up for her. "OK," she said, and tried to smile.

"Meet me here at midnight," said Lillian. "And bring your backpacks."

That night, at 11:30, Lillian snuck out of bed, got dressed, and filled a backpack with granola bars, dried fruit, a flashlight, a steel water bottle, and a pocketknife.

She went downstairs and turned off the porch light so her house would be easier to find. Everyone in Spring Town liked to leave their porch lights on all night. Maisy and Katy knew the way to her house. They knew all the shortcuts, and all the longcuts that they never took, but Lillian turned off the porch light anyway. The darkness made it feel like an adventure.

Maisy sat in her room, packing. She felt excited and happy; she wasn't the tiniest bit scared. Going out at night was nothing new for her. She went on her own adventures all the time: camping in the backyard, reading on the roof, building forts in the park, hanging rope swings from the tallest trees. She always had scuffed elbows, scraped knees, calloused hands, and scabbed knuckles. If her parents found her bed empty in the morning, they wouldn't be worried. "Out on another adventure," they'd say.

Katy searched through her closet. She didn't want to wear a dress because it might get dirty. She gathered her makeup, brush, mirror, and (secretly) her journal.

The journal was covered in painted flowers with a rainbow on top. She turned to a blank page and wrote:

<u>*Going on an Adventure*</u>

I'm forced on an adventure.
Two against one, Maisy always says.

The beach at night is dangerous.
Sharks and crabs and the sound of thunder.

But friendship is stronger than fear.

Katy read her words over a few times. She liked to center her poems in the middle of the page. She felt it looked more professional. She liked everything perfect.

Maisy and Katy walked together to Lillian's house. Katy wore a heavy black coat and skinny jeans. Maisy wore a purple t-shirt and old jeans; she didn't bring a jacket because she didn't mind the cold. They both wore small backpacks filled with supplies for the night.

The street lamps were spaced far apart, leaving big stretches of shadow. Katy thought that a stranger would jump out of every bush and take them. She hid behind Maisy as they walked.

Maisy didn't care that the shadows looked dangerous. She felt excited. She smiled like a Cheshire cat.

Lillian saw two shadows cast by the street lamps, then Maisy and Katy walked across the lawn. Lillian went out to meet them on the grass.

"When we get to the beach, can we have a midnight snack?" asked Maisy.

"Be quiet," hissed Katy. "We don't want Lillian's parents to know what we're doing."

"They won't hear us," said Maisy.

"Whisper anyway!" snapped Katy. She was tired and scared and took it out on Maisy.

Maisy didn't say a word. She didn't like when Katy got mad.

Lillian looked back at her house. With the porch light off, it looked like someone else's home.

Chapter 2. The Mysterious Boy

Lillian, Maisy, and Katy walked down the street. The night was quiet, and they had only the light of the street lamps and the moon, which shone through tangles of branches, making twisted shapes on the ground.

Maisy couldn't stand the silence. "My backpack is heavy. Can't we share *one* backpack?"

"Sure, as long as *you* carry it," said Lillian.

Maisy frowned.

Katy felt scared to go this far from home without her parents' approval. She wanted to go back, but didn't want to be left behind.

They reached the Village area of Spring Town. Maisy wished Bert & Rocky's, the ice cream shop, was open. She would get five scoops of Lem-O-Licious stuffed in a chocolate- and sprinkle-dipped waffle cone. She felt sad just thinking about it.

Lillian looked at the Folk Music Center. Sometimes the workers let her try the fancy harp, the one with a hummingbird drinking out of a flower painted on the side. She loved to play that pretty harp. It sounded like music from another world.

Katy wondered if the Farmers Market would be open in the morning on their way back. She could buy fresh fruit for breakfast. Her favorites were sweet limes (they tasted like water with a hint of sugar), blood oranges (which tasted like any orange but were as red as blood), and mangoes (because they were so sweet).

The clock outside the bank read:

12:25 A.M.
Monday 3-25

It was dark and cold, and Lillian had seen a lot of movies that she now wished she hadn't. She didn't believe in monsters, but they still scared her.

Katy hid behind Maisy and thought about *The Lost World: Jurassic Park*, which she had seen in IMAX 3D. The T-Rex running through town, the bus smashed, the baby T-Rex hunting Peter Ludlow ...

Maisy wasn't scared at all.

Now they were so close to the beach they could hear waves crashing.

It was called Beach of Green Waters because the water looked green in the sun. Now the water was nearly black, reflecting the midnight sky. The full moon danced on the waves.

The beach was almost an island, completely surrounded by water except where large boulders connected it to town. Rough granite steps led down between the boulders.

On the west side of the beach lay Seal Rock, a flat boulder where seals liked to bask in the sun. The townspeople loved to watch the seals, so they built a metal fence to protect the seals from great white sharks. The fence was anchored to the ocean floor and rose eleven feet above the surface of the water. The fence kept the great whites out, but not the thresher sharks, who could leap twenty feet high.

On the east side of the beach, a jetty made out of rocks of different colors and sizes stretched into the ocean. No one walked or fished on the jetty because enormous blue crabs lived there. The jetty used to be called Fisherman's Jetty, until the crabs took over. Everyone called it Crab Jetty now.

The girls walked across the street to a fence that separated the beach from the town. Looking through the chain link, they saw dark boulders going down forty yards, growing smaller and smaller, becoming rocks and then pebbles and then smooth sand.

Ever since Bluebell had disappeared, the beach was closed at night. Three huge locks hung on the gate: one on top, one in the middle, and one on the bottom.

"Oh, well," said Katy. "Guess we'll have to go back."

on their rock, and a shiver of threshers hunted nearby. Wait—was that a boy swimming with the sharks?!

Maisy motioned for Lillian and Katy. They hid behind some boulders and watched as the boy swam through the moonlit water.

The sharks moved in strange patterns around him, fins gliding swiftly through the ocean, leaving silky ripples. The fins were black and bumpy and had pale little scars and rough notches cut out of the backs. The boy kept his head above the water as he swam. Sometimes his hand reached out and touched a shark, who swam out of his way.

The boy walked out of the water. He looked thirteen or fourteen. He wore jeans, a dark green t-shirt, and a gray stone medallion around his neck. Moonlight shone on his golden hair and blue eyes. *His eyes are the color of a summer sky,* thought Katy.

As he scanned the area, the girls ducked behind the boulders. They listened as he walked across the sand. It sounded like he was coming their way.

"The feeling is so strong," whispered Lillian. "I think it's him. I think he's the one calling me."

"That's impossible," said Katy.

"You don't even know him," said Maisy.

"That's true," said a strange voice.

The girls looked up. The boy was leaning against the boulder, looking down at them.

The girls stood and took a cautious step back. The boy looked them over, then focused on Lillian. "I've been waiting for you," he said.

Katy and Maisy exchanged a surprised glance, but Lillian looked him straight in the eye.

"You've been calling me," she said.

"You must be Bluebell's sister," said the boy. "I've been coming here every night for three months trying to find someone who knows Bluebell."

"Why?" asked Lillian. "Where is she?"

"That's a complicated question," said the boy.

Maisy took a step forward and grabbed the boy's shirt in her fist. "Where's Bluebell, surfer dude?"

The boy grinned. "My name's Jack. I can take you to your sister."

Lillian looked at him doubtfully. "I'm Lillian, and this is Katy. The one holding your shirt is Maisy."

"How do we know you're telling the truth?" asked Katy.

"I can show you something that will convince you," said Jack. "But you can't tell anyone what you're about to see."

"Why?" said Maisy, releasing his shirt. "Is it a secret?"

"Yes," said Jack. "A secret that's been kept for thousands of years."

Chapter 3. The Guardian

Jack walked onto the jetty. He picked his way through the crabs, stepping in the empty spaces between their pebbled shells and big open claws. The crabs stirred.

Lillian and Katy watched in amazement. They knew that people dared each other to walk on the Crab Jetty, but no one actually did.

Maisy just looked at the crabs. *Why don't they do something?* she wondered. *I wouldn't just sit there if someone was almost walking on me.*

"I'm going to have to do *that?*" whispered Katy.

"If you touch one of their open claws," said Maisy, "it'll snap shut."

"It's OK," said Jack. "The crabs are my friends. They won't hurt you if you're with me."

Katy looked at Jack to see if he was serious.

"How can a crab be your friend?" said Maisy.

Jack beckoned Katy onto the jetty. She tip-toed, trying to step in the same spaces between the shells and claws. A crab rolled up one eye to glare at her; in the moonlight, the crab looked irate.

"What's the matter with you?" hissed Maisy. "Keep going!" Maisy waited, but Katy didn't answer. "Now what? Did the crab get your tongue?"

"Don't listen to her," said Jack. "Just step in that space to your right."

Katy stepped where Jack pointed and kept going.

Now it was Lillian's turn. She walked on the jetty, cautious to step around the claws. The sound of the waves crashing against the shore made her feel nervous.

Maisy walked through the crabs as if walking through the park.

Jack knelt by a crab the size of a dinner plate. He tapped the crab on the back. The crab rolled up its eyes and, as if recognizing Jack, it moved aside, revealing a small hole in the rock about an inch deep and three inches round. The bottom of the hole was carved with intricate designs of odd flowers and a fierce bird and strange words in a language that the girls couldn't read.

Jack took off his medallion, which was engraved with the same designs as the hole. Lillian pointed to the runes. "What do those say?"

Instead of answering, Jack placed the medallion in the hole. There was a rough sound, like rocks scraping against each other. The crabs scrambled into the water.

The entire jetty shook as the last twenty feet slanted down into the ocean. The water stayed the same level, as if two glass walls kept the sea from spilling over the slanted jetty.

They heard the crunching of rocks and saw the jetty drop down a foot. Further out, it dropped again. Every time it dropped, it formed a stair.

Crunch! Katy watched as the stairs dropped out of sight. Crunch! Maisy felt excited as the steps went deeper and deeper and deeper. Crunch! Lillian watched with a mixture of amazement and fear. Where were the steps leading?

Crunch! Crunch! Crunch!

Katy was about to panic when the noise stopped. She looked down, counting nine steps before the stairs faded into darkness.

"Do we have to go down there?" she asked, trying to stop herself from shaking.

Jack nodded. He walked down the stairs, disappearing into blackness.

Lillian walked cautiously so she wouldn't trip. Maisy strutted down the stairs as if she was in her own house. Then, hesitantly, Katy followed.

The walls were transparent on either side of the stairs. Katy saw sharks and fish swimming in the water beyond. Maisy reached her hand out to feel the invisible wall, but instead of touching a solid surface, her hand went right through into the water. She pulled it back inside.

Lillian and Katy waited. All of a sudden, the pillar shot back up.

Jack touched the elevator and the doors opened. He walked inside, followed by Lillian; Katy walked in more slowly. The doors closed and the elevator dropped. In a few seconds, the elevator stopped moving and the doors opened.

They stepped out onto a stone path. Lamps hung from the rocky ceiling, casting dim blue light from above. The air felt hot. Red light came up from the bottom of either side of the path, mixing into magenta halfway up the walls.

Metal railings stood on both sides of the path. Katy walked in the middle. She didn't want to touch anything. *Where's Maisy?* she thought, looking up the path, worried.

Why is it so hot down here? thought Lillian. She walked over to the railing and saw why … bubbling lava splashed up against the wall six feet below the path. Lillian jumped back in surprise.

"Why is there lava down—" Lillian began.

"Lava?!" Katy yelled. She ran to the edge and grabbed the railing, then quickly snatched her hands back. The railing was hot. She leaned over and stared down at the red lava. She felt like her face had been put in an oven. The heat stirred her hair.

"Why are we down here?! This is danger—"

Katy felt someone push her from behind. She had one horror-filled moment where she thought she was falling, but then was pulled back onto the middle of the path. She whirled around and saw Maisy smiling at her.

Katy swung at Maisy, but Maisy ducked.

"You jerk!" shouted Katy, swinging again.

Maisy hid behind Lillian. "It was a joke!"

Katy advanced on Maisy. "A joke?!"

Maisy pushed Lillian between them.

"We're not here to fight," said Lillian. "We're here to find Bluebell. Katy, you walk in front of me, and you—" she pointed at Maisy, "walk behind me."

Jack led the way, followed by Katy, then Lillian, then Maisy, muttering under her breath.

The dim tunnel was as big as a concert hall. The path was six feet wide and turned left after one hundred feet. The blue light from the lamps high up and the red light from the lava below met at eye level, making a band of magenta that followed the path on both sides. The girls looked around. Everyone felt hot.

Katy tapped Jack on the shoulder. He turned to look at Katy with his bright blue eyes. "Jack, this is really freaking me out. Can this lava erupt? Is this place even safe?"

"Stay in the middle of the path," Jack reassured her, "and you'll be fine."

Where's Bluebell? thought Lillian. *Why would she come down here? How did she even find this place?* She didn't know what to think, but she told herself over and over, *You cannot act scared.* She didn't show it, but she secretly *was* scared. She had the strangest feeling someone was watching them.

Then they heard something. On one side of the railing, the lava began making a hissing noise.

"Don't worry," said Jack. "That's just the Guardian. He won't hurt you if you're with me."

The sound of rusty metal rubbing against rock grew louder, moving up toward them.

A big metal robot, over one hundred feet tall, climbed out of the lava. It had five spikes on its head, two red square eyes, and a rectangular mouth. Four arms, bolted to the thick, rusty, gray body, moved toward Jack and the girls. Instead of hands, each of the arms ended in a weapon: a long sword for the top right hand, a sharp spike for the top left, a metal club for the bottom right, and a three-digit claw for the bottom left.

Jack waved a greeting at the robot.

But instead of waving back, the robot's claw dropped toward Katy. She tried to dodge, but the claw closed around her like she was a toy in a claw machine. Katy screamed. The monster looked at her like it was trying to decide what to do.

Lillian stepped toward the robot. "Katy!"

Maisy turned to Jack. "Don't worry?!"

The sword on the robot's arm swung toward them. The sword was twelve feet long and one foot wide. Maisy dropped to the floor, pulling Lillian down with her. As it sliced the air, the wind from the sword swirled their hair.

Lillian watched the sword sweep toward Jack like a reaper's scythe. "Watch out!"

But Jack ran *toward* the sword … and jumped. He landed on the moving blade, wobbling as he tried to keep his balance. He ran up the sword onto the arm. The robot held Katy over its head while swinging its club-hand at Jack. It missed and made a small dent in its own arm. It kept swinging the club and missing, making human-sized dents in itself.

The robot's eyes got redder as it got madder. It swung at Jack as he ran over its shoulder. As the robot turned, the girls saw Katy trying to squeeze out of the claw.

Lillian stood up. "Katy!"

Maisy pulled her back down as the robot swung its club just above their heads. "Maybe we could worry about ourselves right now!"

Maisy lifted her head and saw Jack running up the robot's shoulder. "What's he doing?"

This time, Lillian pulled Maisy down as the club swung through the space where her head had just been.

Jack climbed up the robot until he reached its head. He pushed on the middle spike, which slid forward, revealing a dark passageway. A ladder led down into the robot. Jack climbed inside.

Lillian and Maisy ran toward the elevator, chased by the robot. Its huge legs pushed through the boiling lava.

Inside, Jack looked around. It was dim and hotter

than outside. Slow-moving, rusty escalators climbed in every direction. Jack raced down one of the escalators, which ended at a control platform. On the curved wall were levers and switches. In the center floated a small glass chamber that sparked with a ball of golden energy. A round shape was embedded in the glass.

Meanwhile, Lillian and Maisy reached the place where the elevator had been. But it had gone back up.

Maisy kicked the wall. "We need the stupid medallion to get the elevator back!"

They heard the robot getting closer.

At the control panel, Jack took off his medallion. He held it against the glass.

Maisy and Lillian pressed their backs against the rock wall. The robot leaned over the rail. Its head, about the size of a garbage truck, slowly lowered until it was level with the girls. They stared into the big red eyes. The robot pressed closer, as if it was going to squish them against the wall—then stopped, only inches away.

"What happened?" said Lillian.

"Who cares?" said Maisy. She pulled Lillian away from the wall. "Let's go."

As they ran, they saw Jack climbing down the back of the robot. The claw that held Katy slowly lowered. Lillian and Maisy helped pull her out. Katy was pale and trembling. Her arms looked bruised.

Maisy whipped around to glare at Jack. "The robot won't *hurt* us?! It almost *killed* us!"

"I don't understand," said Jack. "The Guardian never attacked me before."

"I want to go home," said Katy.

Lillian put a comforting hand on Katy's shoulder. "You're right, let's go home."

Jack looked at Lillian closely. "I'll show you the way out."

He turned and walked down the path away from the elevator, lava on either side. The girls exchanged a worried glance.

"Is this the way home?" called Lillian.

Jack didn't answer. He just walked on. The girls had no choice but to follow.

Chapter 4. Rattle in the Dark

The girls followed Jack along the path. Turning a corner, they saw that the path ended at a wall thirty feet ahead.

"It's a dead end," said Katy.

Maisy laughed. "Chill out! Don't you see the hole for Jack's medallion?"

Before Katy could reply, they heard noises from around the corner behind them. It sounded like a scurry of squirrels chattering after taking a big breath of helium.

They all turned, listening. The gibbering noise grew louder and closer.

Suddenly, hundreds of brown fluffy balls the size of hedgehogs tumbled around the corner, jostling toward Jack and the girls. Their small black eyes were shiny like a stuffed animal's, and their flattened bulldog noses gave them a cute appearance. Their faces were so furry that the girls couldn't see their mouths. The creatures rushed toward them in a brown tide.

Katy stepped nervously behind Jack. "What are those things?"

"Brownies," said Jack. "But they're different from the brownies you might find in your house."

"Yeah," said Maisy sarcastically, "I see brownies all the time in my house."

Lillian knelt down. "They're so cute."

"They're harmless," Jack shrugged.

Lillian picked one up. It was as light as a baby chick. She ran her fingers over it. The brownie fussed and struggled to get away. "These things are almost all fur."

Then another brownie hopped onto her tennis shoe and climbed up her jeans, followed by another and another. Their feet were the size of peanuts, with three monkey-like toes. Their hands were a little smaller, with four fingers on each. Their toes and fingers were sticky, like a gecko's.

Lillian looked down and saw at least fifteen brownies climbing up her pants. She was so surprised she dropped the brownie she was holding. It floated to the ground, then climbed up her leg too.

Now the brownies were climbing over everyone, a slow swarm of fuzzy brown.

"Leave me alone!" shrieked Katy, shaking her legs vigorously. "Why aren't these things coming off!"

Maisy laughed. The brownies covered her up to

the waist. She tried to pull them off, but they stuck, stretching her clothes as she yanked them in different directions. "Get off, you maniacal fur balls!"

Lillian felt like she was wearing a brownie suit up to her chest. She tried to tug them off but they clung on. She looked right: Maisy and Katy struggled with the same problem. She looked left: a pile of brownies were trying to climb up Jack's legs, but they only got to his knees before they slipped and tumbled down.

Brownies pulled on the girls' hair, scrabbled under their coats, yanked on their pockets, gibbered in their ears, and jumped on their heads.

"Get off, you ninnies!" shouted Maisy.

"Don't climb on my face!" Katy screamed.

Lillian was completely covered with brownies. "Help!" she shouted, her voice muffled by all the fur.

The girls could still breathe, but the brownies' feet felt weird on their faces, like bunches of soft stickers pressed on and peeled off.

I have to do something, thought Jack—when suddenly, all the brownies scurried off the girls in a rush and stampeded away as fast as their little legs could take them. In a matter of seconds, they were gone.

The girls stood stunned and amazed.

"Why did they leave?" asked Lillian.

Katy took off her backpack and removed a mirror. She checked to see if there were any brownies in her hair. "I don't care why they left. I'm just glad they're gone."

Jack didn't look happy. "Brownies don't just run away without a reason—"

"Look!" pointed Maisy. "That brownie ran in the wrong direction! I'm gonna get you!" She sprinted after the lone brownie.

Katy turned to Lillian. "Maisy has no self-control."

"She'll never catch it," said Jack.

Lillian sighed. "We better go after her."

Maisy chased the brownie all the way to the wall, but the brownie squeezed under the door and was gone. She kicked the stone door. The thud echoed ominously.

Jack and the girls ran up.

"Don't do that," said Jack.

"Do what?!" snapped Maisy.

Jack lowered his voice. "Make loud noises."

Maisy raised her voice even louder. "Why not?! Why shouldn't I be loud?! The robot was loud and you didn't seem to care!"

"Because," warned Jack, "brownies aren't the only creatures down here. Something has changed since I brought Bluebell. This place isn't safe anymore."

Katy did a double-take. "There are *more* monsters down here?"

Jack nodded. "This may get more dangerous."

"I'm going home," said Katy, turning around.

"Party pooper," grouched Maisy under her breath.

Katy spun back. "This isn't a party! This is life and death! My life! My death!"

Jack put a finger to his lips.

He took off his medallion and pressed it into the round hole. The door slowly scraped upward, disappearing into a slot in the ceiling. They walked through the threshold—BOOM! The door crashed down behind them.

Katy and Lillian jumped at the echoing noise.

"So much for being quiet," said Maisy.

"Is this the way out?" asked Katy.

The railing still ran along the left side of the path, but the right side was an uneven stone wall that climbed up to the ceiling. The path ran thirty feet ahead, then curved out of sight.

As they walked, Lillian noticed a stone the size of a baseball on the ground.

She picked it up. "This stone is an odd shape. It has all these lines in it. Almost like fur." She turned the gray stone slowly in her hand—and saw a face looking back at her. She dropped the stone in surprise. It broke into several pieces. "It's a statue of a brownie!"

They heard a noise, like a rattlesnake, but much louder. The girls felt a chill seep down into their minds. They turned to Jack. For the first time, Jack looked worried too.

The noise grew louder, moving toward them.

"What's making that weird sound?" asked Maisy. She took a step along the path.

Jack grabbed her by the shoulder. "Look down and close your eyes."

"What?" snapped Maisy.

Lillian and Katy stared at Jack.

"Now!" Jack commanded.

The girls looked down at their feet.

"And close your eyes!"

They shut their eyes. Katy felt Jack snatch the mirror out of her hand.

In the gloom of their closed eyes, the sound got louder as it turned the corner.

"What is that?" whispered Lillian.

The noise paused just beyond the turn. Five feet up the wall, Jack saw several small snakes peek around the corner. The snakes were different colors—red, blue, green, and brown. Hissing loudly, they moved up and down and side to side, their small, emotionless eyes hunting the area.

Then the rest of the creature slithered around the corner. She had snakes instead of hair and a monstrous woman's face with gray-green, scaly skin. Rags hung from her shoulders. She held a large wood bow in one hand, and a quiver of arrows on her back with a leather strap across her chest. Her bottom half was a snake, ending in a rattle. She used a clawed hand to drag herself along the ground. Her yellow eyes found Jack.

Medusa, he thought, his heart sinking. *What's she doing here?*

"Keep your eyes closed," he repeated to the girls.

Katy and Maisy listened, but Lillian was too curious. Without looking up, she opened her eyes. On the rocky path she saw a strangely familiar shadow, like a nest of snakes writhing on the ground. She recognized it from her favorite Ray Harryhausen movie. *Medusa?* she thought, shutting her eyes. *But monsters aren't real!*

Lillian would have been surprised to see Jack look Medusa in the eye and not turn to stone. Medusa's nostrils flared and her red lips grimaced, revealing sharp, broken teeth.

The rattle grew louder as Medusa pulled herself closer. She reached back over her shoulder, grabbed an arrow, nocked it in place, drew the bowstring and, to Jack's surprise, aimed at Lillian.

Medusa released the arrow. Jack spun Lillian out of the way, toward the wall. Lillian opened her eyes in surprise as the arrow shot through her curly red hair. The bottom of her hair sizzled, withered all the way up to her shoulders, became ash, and drifted away.

"Eyes closed!" yelled Jack.

He whipped around. Medusa had another arrow, this one aimed at him. She opened her reptilian hand, the bowstring sang and the shaft cut through the air, its arrowhead green with poison.

Jack threw his hand up. The arrow was on course for his heart, but curved around his hand and embedded in the wall between Maisy and Katy. They jumped, but kept their eyes closed.

The air between Jack and Medusa thickened like water. Medusa's face looked like it was rippling through the air. She seemed surprised and upset that Jack could conjure such a defense.

Jack looked back at the girls. He knew that if he didn't do something right now, they all could be killed. Medusa scared Jack; he didn't want to fight her, but there was nothing else to do.

He pushed through the wall. Medusa shot another arrow but Jack turned sideways, the arrow only inches from hitting him. It sped through the rippling wall, curved, and narrowly missed Katy, who screamed but kept her eyes shut tight.

Jack ran toward Medusa. She dropped her bow and pulled an arrow out of her quiver. Holding it like a dagger, she slithered to meet Jack. She thrust the arrow at his chest, but Jack stepped to the side. She slashed at his neck. Jack was too quick; he ducked out of the way. Medusa grew more angry and swung the arrow more wildly. Jack dodged back out of her murderous reach.

Finally she lunged at him, stabbing with all her might. This time, Jack slipped to one side, grabbed the wooden shaft with his right hand, and snapped it with the heel of his left. Now Jack had a weapon too.

Lillian heard noises. She had to peek. Through the wall of thick air she saw Medusa battling Jack. It looked like a scene out of *Clash of the Titans*.

How can Jack look at Medusa and not turn to stone? she wondered. *What's he doing? Why is the air rippling like that?*

"Look," she whispered.

Katy opened her eyes. "Medusa? That's impossible!"

Maisy looked up. "Medusa? That's awesome!"

"That's not awesome," whispered Katy "Medusa is a myth. This is impossible. She's not real."

"Looks real to me," said Maisy.

Medusa advanced on Jack. He pulled Katy's mirror out of his pocket and held it up to Medusa's face. The monster stopped abruptly, staring at her reflection. As part of her curse, whenever Medusa looked into a mirror she saw herself as the beautiful girl she had once been. Her reflection had long brown hair, brown eyes, and smooth skin.

For just a moment, Medusa gazed at herself sadly. But that was all Jack needed to slip behind her and press the arrow to her throat. Medusa's snakes spun toward Jack, and Medusa jerked her hand toward the arrow—but Jack pressed the poisoned tip harder against her throat. Snakes hovered inches from his face, ready to bite.

Jack dropped Katy's mirror, which shattered on the floor. With his free hand, he covered Medusa's eyes.

"Run!" he ordered, but the girls just stood dumbfounded as the watery wall faded.

"Run!" shouted Jack.

The girls jumped, then ran past Medusa and Jack. Maisy stopped and took a step toward Medusa, but Lillian pulled her away.

"Come on!" said Maisy. "How many times do you get a chance to touch Medusa?!"

Lillian pulled her around the corner with Katy.

The girls stopped running. They were in a cul-de-sac of rock.

"It's a dead end!" said Katy.

They searched the walls but there was no hole for Jack's medallion—which meant no door and no elevator.

"Well," said Maisy, "looks like I'll get to touch Medusa after all."

Jack waited another few seconds to make sure the girls were well around the corner … then spun away and sprinted. He heard Medusa's rattle behind him, and the hiss of her snakes. He grabbed her bow with his right hand and took off his medallion with his left. He raced around the corner.

"What's happening?!" shouted Katy.

Jack didn't answer. He ran to the middle of the cul-de-sac, bent down and pressed the medallion in a hole at his feet. The floor of the entire cul-de-sac suddenly descended, scraping against the rocky walls. Lillian and Katy looked around in surprise and took a couple of steps away from the wall.

"This is so awesome!" exclaimed Maisy.

They all watched the opening above get smaller and smaller. Then they heard the chilling sound of a rattle.

"Close your eyes," said Jack.

The girls shut their eyes.

Jack looked up. He saw Medusa peer over the edge, more furious than ever. She took an arrow from her quiver and threw it with so much force it stuck in the ground at Jack's feet. The poison turned the stone around it a rotten shade of black.

Part Two

LANODEKA

Chapter 5. From Beneath the Sea

The elevator stopped with a jolt. "You can look now," Jack said.

The girls opened their eyes. Before them stood a tunnel. They rushed in, glad to leave all the monsters behind. Jack glanced back up at Medusa. She glared at him, her snakes moving wildly, snapping at the air.

Dropping Medusa's big bow, Jack turned and followed the girls into the tunnel. Sunlight glowed at the end, fifty yards away. The girls raced toward the light and came out onto a sunny beach.

"Home!" shouted Katy. "Thank goodness!"

Lillian and Maisy looked out at the ocean.

"If this was home," said Maisy, "it'd be night. Where's Seal Rock? Where's Crab Jetty? Where's the town?"

"Welcome to Lanodeka," said Jack with a smile.

The bright blue sky felt bigger, the smooth yellow sand sparkled like the sun, and the ocean water seemed too clear. "I thought you said this was the way home," said Katy.

"Actually," said Jack. "I said I'd lead us out ... of the tunnel."

"That's a dirty trick," said Maisy.

"Are we still *underground?*" asked Lillian.

"Are you crazy?" said Maisy. "Can you have the sky underground? Can you have the sun and an ocean underground?"

"Actually," said Jack, "we *are* underground."

Maisy rapped on Jack's head with her knuckles. "Medusa must have paralyzed your brain."

"I hate to agree with Maisy," said Katy, "but how can we be underground?"

"I don't know how to describe what I'm feeling," Lillian thought out loud. "This place feels ... familiar."

Jack turned toward the ocean. Small waves tumbled on the sand. "Lanodeka was built by the monsters who live here. Thousands of years ago, people hunted the monsters almost to extinction. So they left the human world and built one of their own."

"You mean," said Katy, "we're trapped in a world of monsters?"

"Awesome!" said Maisy.

"But that's isn't possible," said Katy. "You can't just *make* worlds!"

Maisy took a look around. "Looks made to me."

Lillian gazed at the vast ocean and wondered, *Where is my sister in this strange world?*

Jack, Lillian, and Maisy walked along the shore. They felt warm water wash over their shoes. Katy didn't want to get her shoes wet, so she stood away from the surf.

Jack took off his medallion and threw it as far as he could.

"What are you doing?" called Katy. "Aren't we going to need that to get back?"

The medallion flipped end over end and hit the water with an unexpected *boom!* Ripples pulsed outward, sending a tremor through the sand.

Lillian ran out of the water to stand with Katy.

"Did you feel that?" Lillian whispered.

They watched as something white appeared where Jack's medallion sank. It looked like a shark swimming toward them, but when it rose to the surface, they saw it was a small boat.

The boat glided forward. In a few seconds a small wave pushed it to shore and the hull made a scraping sound as it rubbed against the sand. The slim boat looked weathered, as if it had been through hundreds of storms. The white paint was chipped and blistered in several places. Two warped benches stretched across the middle. Jack's medallion lay at the bottom.

Jack stepped into the boat and picked up his medallion. He sat down on one of the benches.

"I don't want to get into that old boat," said Katy.

"Would you rather swim across the ocean?" asked Maisy pleasantly.

"No," said Katy.

"Do you want to stay here?"

"No."

"Then do you want to get in the stinkin' boat?!"

"Yes," murmured Katy.

Katy walked down to the water, careful not to get her shoes wet. But there was a puddle at the bottom of the boat, and water sloshed over her shoes as she climbed in. She sighed and sat down next to Jack.

Lillian stood by the boat. "Where are we going?"

"To the other side," said Jack.

"It'll take weeks to cross."

"Actually, the ocean isn't as big as it looks."

"It looks pretty big to me," said Katy.

"Yeah," said Maisy. "Whoever heard of a small ocean?"

"It's more like a lake," Jack shrugged.

Maisy looked at the ocean. All she saw was water. "If it was a lake, we could see the other side."

"You can't see the other side of Lake Michigan," observed Katy.

"Where's Lake Michigan?" said Maisy.

"Don't you ever do your geography homework?"

"Stop it," said Lillian as she climbed into the boat. She sat next to Maisy. "I know this is kind of scary, but it looks like we have to keep going. And we have to stick together. Are you ready?"

"Yes!" grinned Maisy.

"Ready as I'll ever be," said Katy.

"OK," said Jack. "Lets go."

"How are we gonna go anywhere without oars?" asked Maisy.

As if in answer to her question, the boat glided away from the shore and into the big blue.

The boat moved slowly at first. Then it gained speed, moving steadily faster and faster until the prow tilted up out of the water. The wind whipped through their hair, and ocean spray showered their faces.

Katy took off her backpack and groped inside. She yanked out a compact umbrella, pushed it open and hid behind it. The water splattered like rain against the pink fabric.

"You bring everything," said Maisy. "This is fun! Close your umbrella and enjoy the warm ocean water!"

"Enjoy!" exclaimed Katy. "Enjoy! I'm not enjoying this at all!"

Maisy snatched the umbrella and closed it.

"Look!" said Lillian. "Dolphins!"

Fifty yards away, scores of dolphins arced out of the water and sliced back in. The water around them churned white as they surged through the choppy waves. As the dolphins leapt, they shone with a variety of hues. Some were green, others were blue or purple; some were even pink. It looked like a rainbow weaving through the water.

"Why are they different colors?" asked Lillian.

"Because," said Maisy, "they're not dolphins."

"Then what are they?" asked Katy.

Jack hesitated.

"Why won't you tell us anything?" demanded Lillian. "You wait and let us find out what's coming. Why can't you tell us in advance?"

"If you'd rather know," said Jack, "they're sirens."

"Oh," said Katy—then did a double take. "When you say sirens, do you mean evil mermaids?"

"Sirens aren't evil," said Jack.

Before he could explain, Lillian put her finger to her lips. "Do you hear that?"

Everyone listened closely. They heard singing. The voices harmonized, all different ranges and pitches, growing louder and softer as sirens jumped in and out of the water, reverberating and blending into one lovely sound.

"They have the most beautiful voices I've ever heard," said Lillian.

The song grew louder as the sirens passed.

Maisy looked at Jack curiously. "If they're sirens, why aren't they affecting you? Aren't guys supposed to go berserk when they hear the siren's call?"

Two sirens broke away from the group and swam toward the boat. As they jumped in and out of the water, the girls could see their faces. One had purple hair with blue eyes, dark skin, and a green tail. The other had pink hair, pink eyes, pale skin, and a pink tail.

Katy stared. *They're so pretty!*

One of the sirens grabbed onto the edge of the boat while the other dove down and popped up on the other side.

"Hello, Jack," said the siren with purple hair.

"Where have you been, Jack?" asked the one with pink hair.

"Did you leave *our* world again?"

"Did you bring us a gift from the *human* world?"

Maisy raised her eyebrows at Jack. "You're friends with sirens?"

The purple-haired siren smiled impishly. "You haven't told them, Jack?"

"Told us what?" demanded Maisy.

"Keeping secrets again, Jack?" added the pink-haired one.

"You told Bluebell when you brought *her* down here, Jack."

Maisy crossed her arms. "Tell us what?!"

Both sirens lowered themselves so only their eyes peeked over the edges of the boat. "He's a siren!" They laughed, dove backward with a splash, and disappeared.

"You're a *siren?*" blurted Katy.

"Is that why you could look at Medusa?" Lillian asked.

Katy touched Jack's arm. "Why didn't you tell us?"

Maisy looked over the edge of the boat to watch the sirens swim away. "Uh, guys. I think you'll want to see this."

Jack and the girls looked down into the clear water.

A giant eye was moving toward the surface. The eye was perfectly round and the size of a whale. As the massive head turned, they saw a second eye. Both fixed on the boat.

Katy stared with growing terror. "What is that?!"

As the eye rose closer to the boat, they saw it was attached to something big and purple. The monster looked like a giant octopus with dozens of tentacles.

Lillian glanced around. "What should we do?"

"Jump!" shouted Jack, and dove into the water.

Katy stared after him. "Is he crazy?!"

Lillian and Maisy jumped, but Katy didn't move. "They're crazy too!"

Katy looked back down into the clear water. The monster's two huge eyes took up most of its face, and below the eyes Katy saw a row of sharp teeth. The behemoth had two pointy ears about twenty feet long and shiny, rubbery skin. All of its tentacles undulated, propelling itself upwards.

The creature's green eyes stared right at Katy. The purple eyelids slid shut and opened again. Horrified, Katy stepped away from the side of the boat. As she tried to step back again, her legs hit the other edge, her ams flailed, and she tumbled backwards with a scream, splashing into the water.

Katy bobbed to the surface, rubbed her eyes and looked around. The monster erupted out of the sea.

Water splashed in every direction, huge whitecaps swamping the area. One of the waves thrust Katy away. Other waves reached Jack, Lillian, and Maisy, and forced them further from the monster.

The girls stared up at it. Katy swam toward them. "What *is* that?" she gasped.

The creature's purple head was as big as an island. Its huge green eyes scanned the area. Underneath the water, its tentacles moved back and forth. Big swells reached Jack and the girls, making them bob up and down.

"The Kraken," said Jack darkly.

The Kraken raised a tentacle out of the water and slammed it down. Crash! The sound echoed as bits of the boat flew around them. Hunks of sharp wood shot past Jack and the girls. More huge waves pushed them further from the Kraken.

The Kraken's eyes moved slowly, side to side, and then looked down at them. Its green irises were so huge that even from forty yards away, Jack and the girls saw their own terrified reflections.

Out of the corner of her eye, Lillian saw movement in the water below. She looked down past her own legs treading water and saw scores of tentacles writhing like snakes, rising toward them.

Lillian stopped treading water, spellbound by the tentacles below. As she sank a few inches, water filled her mouth. She spat out the salty liquid.

"Jack!" she sputtered. "Maisy! Katy! Look down!"

Everyone looked and saw tentacles right under their feet. Maisy kicked at one. The bottom of her tennis shoe stuck to the rubbery, viscous skin and instantly Maisy was yanked underwater. Lillian and Katy stared at the spot where she disappeared.

With a whoosh the tentacle burst out of the sea, Maisy dangling off of it, upside down. She spat and coughed and flailed, sixty feet in the air, jerking her foot and screaming curses that no one could make out.

"Do something!" Katy shouted at Jack.

Before anyone could react, they heard a shout. They looked up and saw Maisy falling. She had slipped out of her tennis shoe and now tumbled through the air, plummeting back toward the ocean. She curled up into a cannonball and hit the water with a loud splash. She sank for a few seconds before opening her eyes. She stared up through a moving mass of dark tentacles to the bright wavering sky. Maisy swam carefully through the spongy coils to the surface. She gasped for air.

"Maisy!" cried Lillian. "Are you OK?!"

Katy threw her arms around Maisy, pushing Maisy back underwater. Maisy shoved Katy away and bobbed back to the surface. She splashed water at Katy. "Are you trying to drown me?!"

"The Kraken could have killed you!"

Something white bobbed out of the water and floated on the surface.

Lillian pointed. "The boat!"

"But that's impossible!" said Katy.

"It's magic," said Jack. "A new boat will rise out of the water wherever the old one sinks."

The boat glided toward them, as if knowing they needed it.

"We're safe!" huffed Katy, out of breath from treading water.

The girls watched the boat race toward them. They felt hope fill their lungs like air.

But the boat sped right past.

Maisy turned to Jack. "Yeah, nice magic."

They watched the boat glide away.

"What's that?" asked Lillian.

Beyond the boat, the water was bubbling and white, rushing toward them like a crashing wave.

"As if things weren't bad enough," said Maisy.

"I can't tread water much longer," whispered Katy.

As the roiling wave rolled closer, they saw it wasn't a wave at all. The water was crowded with sirens, arcing out of the ocean and splashing back in.

The sirens are helping the Kraken! thought Lillian.

Before Jack and the girls could do anything, the sirens swarmed around them. Lillian and Katy ducked underwater and saw hundreds of sirens below them, swimming so fast that their colorful hair and dolphin tails shimmered. It was the kind of sight that turned fear into wonder. Even Katy, for that moment, felt happy.

The girls floated to the surface. Scores of sirens

jumped overhead, tails shining in the sun, water sprinkling down like rain.

Maisy stared up at the sirens, eyes wild with exhilaration. She reached out her hand and touched the sirens' tails as they dove over. Their skin felt as slick as fish. "I touched a siren!"

Jack and the girls turned to watch as the sirens sped toward the Kraken.

"What are they doing?" asked Lillian.

"Helping us," said Jack.

Katy looked happy but confused. "Why?"

The sirens came at the Kraken in one huge group. The Kraken raised a large tentacle and brought it down hard, slapping the surface of the water, but the sirens scattered out of reach. Then the Kraken lifted dozens of tentacles and crashed them down at the same time. The ocean exploded, and a huge wave swept Jack and the girls back, flipping and tumbling. When Lillian resurfaced, she found herself facing away from the Kraken.

"The boat!" she shouted.

Everyone looked and saw another siren swimming toward them, pulling the white boat behind her.

"Come on," said Jack.

The siren held the boat steady. Jack grabbed onto the side and pulled himself in. Maisy hooked her foot on the edge, heaved up, and then flopped over. Jack bent down, grabbed Katy under her arms, and lifted her out of the water. Katy stared into Jack's eyes. *His eyes are so blue,* she thought.

Meanwhile, Maisy pulled Lillian's arm.

"Just do what I did!" she said. "Get your foot on the edge!"

Finally, Lillian fell into the boat. At that moment, the siren released the boat and it glided away. The girls turned to watch the havoc between the sirens and the Kraken shrink in the distance.

Katy sighed. "I can't believe we made it."

Everyone laughed, relieved to be alive.

Chapter 6. Mysterious World

Lillian saw something in the distance. "Look!" she shouted. "Land!"

Everyone turned and saw the far shore. Its beauty transfixed them. A forest of high green trees ended at foothills that climbed into tall mountains. The snowy peaks looked like sparkling white hats. Just above, a radiant, full moon shone in a dark sky scattered with stars. A river of transparent water gently flowed down through the woods. To the west, an immense waterfall seemed to fall from heaven. Even from a distance, Jack and the girls heard it rumble into the ocean.

"It's like a dream," whispered Lillian.

"How can it be night way out there over the mountains," said Maisy, pointing one hand at the full moon, "but still be day here, over the sea?" she added, pointing her other hand straight up at the sun.

As usual, Jack didn't answer.

Everyone watched as the shore grew closer. The boat scraped as it bumped onto the sand. Maisy jumped out first, followed by Lillian, Katy, and Jack. They heard the boat scuff. Turning, they saw it glide away.

The sand became smoother as they walked away from the water.

"I'm hungry," said Katy, reaching for her backpack. Then she remembered it was on the bottom of the ocean.

They sat in the shade of a large tree at the edge of the forest. In the distance, Lillian saw the waterfall crashing down on the shore. She craned her neck to see the source, but the water fell from the sky itself. Or rather, it seemed to fall *through* the sky from a higher source. *That's the most amazing thing I've ever seen.*

She looked up at the tree they were sitting under. As wide as a Sequoia, it towered at least one hundred feet high and ended in a wall of leaves in all shades of green.

Lillian gazed into the forest. She saw a few bushes and tree trunks, and more tree trunks. As she stared deeper into the forest, it grew darker and darker until she couldn't see anything at all. Lillian felt a chill. There was nothing comforting about this forest. She listened but couldn't hear anything, and nothing moved.

"I wish I'd brought a change of clothes," said Katy, taking off her jacket and wringing it out. "But I thought we'd be home in the morning."

"It wouldn't have mattered," said Maisy. "We lost our backpacks." She scanned the area. "Is there anything to eat here?"

Katy pointed at the ocean. "What's that?"

Something was moving fast toward shore, leaving a trail of white water behind it. As it got closer, they saw it was a siren. The beautiful pink-haired creature threw several things into the waves.

"Our backpacks!" shouted Katy.

"My shoe!" crowed Maisy, laughing as the siren threw a tennis shoe onto the sand.

The girls ran to the shore and grabbed their backpacks. Everyone but Maisy checked to see if anything was damaged by the water. Maisy found a granola bar, tore the wrapper open and munched on it happily as she walked toward Jack.

Katy opened her backpack, unzipped a small pocket, reached in and pulled out a key. Then she opened a waterproof compartment and there was her journal, dry as could be.

Lillian and Katy followed Maisy back up the shore. Katy walked to a tree a few yards away from the group. She sat down, unlocked her journal, took out a pen, and wrote:

> *I'm on a dangerous adventure,*
> *with monsters like Krakens and sirens.*
> *I want this adventure to end.*
> *I want to forget this ever happened.*
> *I want to go home, where I'm safe.*

Lillian grabbed an apple out of her backpack and took a bite. The apple tasted sweeter than sugar.

"How can she bring a journal on an adventure?" whispered Maisy.

"Don't judge," said Lillian.

Maisy crossed her arms. "I like judging people."

"Come on, Maisy. You know you love Katy."

"Since when?"

"Since we were little—"

Maisy put a finger to her lips. "Shhh! She's coming."

Katy locked her journal, put it into its waterproof compartment and hid the key. She joined the picnic of granola bars and fruit. She offered some to Jack.

Maisy yawned. "I'm tired."

It was still daytime over the ocean and forest. The sun hadn't descended any lower since they entered this world. *And if I could see the mountains,* thought Lillian, *I bet it's still night there.*

She looked at her watch. "It's five in the morning."

Katy looked worried. "My parents will be waking up soon."

"When does the sun set in this chaotic world?" asked Maisy.

"It never sets," explained Jack. "When they made this part of the world, they made it always day."

"Why?" asked Katy.

"Because the monsters who live deep in the ocean, where it's dark, don't want it to be dark when they come up to the surface."

"But from the boat we saw the moon."

"The creatures who live in the mountains don't like the sun. A lot of them live in caves. So they made that part of the world always night."

"But that's scientifically impossible," said Lillian. "With orbits and gravity, the sun and the moon can't stay in the same place."

Jack shrugged. "The monsters made this world with magic, Lillian."

"I'm tired of hearing the word *magic!*" said Maisy.

"Fine," said Jack with a smile. "They made this world with wizardry, sorcery, spells, curses, charms, and enchantments."

Lillian and Katy laughed.

Maisy tried not to smile. "Shut up, Mr. Thesaurus. I'm going to sleep."

"Yeah," said Jack. "We all need to get some shuteye, forty winks, a snooze, a siesta, a little slumber—"

"Let me put this in a way you can understand," Maisy interrupted. "Dummy up, pipe down, shut your trap, and put a lid on it."

For the first time since the adventure started, everyone laughed together. They were becoming friends with Jack.

The girls settled down in the shade of a big tree. Lillian lay on her back, facing a sky of leaves. The same thoughts kept drifting through her mind. *Where's Bluebell? Why would she want to come here? How did she even know about this place? Why doesn't she come home? Doesn't she miss us?*

All these questions made Lillian's heart feel as heavy as a rock in her chest. She drifted into an uneasy sleep.

Katy took a pink, plastic square out of her backpack. She unfolded it and blew into the corner until it inflated into a pillow. She lay on her side, hugging the firm pillow. *I wish monsters weren't real,* she thought. *I wish this place wasn't real. Lillian's my friend, and I want to help her, but this is more than I bargained for. I don't want to die here.* She fell into a sleep of bad dreams.

Maisy pretended to be asleep. She watched until Katy was breathing heavily, then slowly lifted Katy's head with one hand, pulled the pillow out with the other, and eased Katy's head to the ground. She looked up and saw Jack watching her.

"She'll never miss it," whispered Maisy.

Jack just shook his head.

Maisy lay her head on Katy's pillow. She closed her eyes and, without a worry in the world, fell asleep.

Jack kept watch. *Things have changed since Bluebell came here,* he thought. *I hope Lillian can help us make things right.*

Maisy woke first. She carefully lifted Katy's head and slid the pillow back under it. She looked up. Again, Jack was watching her. She gave him the stink eye.

The girls woke a few minutes later. The sun was still in the same place, shining in the blue sky.

They yawned and stretched. Lillian opened her backpack and took out a pear for breakfast. Maisy unzipped her backpack, reached in and grabbed a granola bar. She ripped open the wrapper and took a huge bite. While she chewed, she took out all the food she had and laid it out like she was dealing cards.

"What are you doing?" asked Lillian.

Maisy smiled. "Eating breakfast."

"We were only supposed to be gone a few hours," said Katy. "You always bring too much."

"Said the girl who brought an umbrella," Maisy smirked. "I like to eat, OK?"

"We need to ration our food," said Lillian. "We don't know how long we'll be here."

"Fine," said Maisy, frowning. She picked up one granola bar and held it out to Lillian.

Instead of taking the bar, Lillian leaned forward and scooped up the rest of Maisy's food. "You can have the granola bar." Lillian tossed Maisy's food into her own backpack for safekeeping.

Maisy dropped her head in mock despair. "What else is there to eat in this stupid world?"

"There's fruit in the forest," said Jack. "But I don't know if you'll like it."

"Great," said Maisy. "We're going to starve."

"You mean that Lillian and I will starve," said Katy. "Maisy, you eat *anything*. By the time we're through the forest, there won't be any food left."

Everyone but Maisy laughed.

"Very funny, you," said Maisy.

Katy felt around in her backpack for dried fruit.

"Now where do we go?" asked Lillian.

Maisy pointed to the waterfall. "Can we go there?"

"We could," said Jack, "but going through the forest is faster."

Everyone started packing up.

"The forest is faster, ration your food," Maisy mimicked under her breath. "I thought America was a free country. Oh yeah, this isn't America."

"What are you muttering?" asked Lillian.

"Nothing," said Maisy as she zipped up her backpack.

Everyone walked into the forest except Maisy. She stood looking down into the river.

"There's a rivermander in there," Jack warned.

"A what?" asked Maisy. She gazed into the river, the water as transparent as water in a drinking glass, the bottom covered with small, smooth, round pebbles like red and purple beads. "What are you talking about? There's nothing here."

"Don't go near it," warned Jack.

Maisy ignored him. She reached into the river and took a red and purple pebble. The pebble felt cold in her fingers.

Maisy smirked at Jack. "See, I got my pebble and a monster didn't attack me."

Then Maisy saw something move in the river. The stones seemed to be shifting. It looked like the outline of a huge alligator. It swam toward her.

Maisy pointed. "What's that?"

"The rivermander you said wasn't there," said Jack.

Lillian and Katy stepped toward Maisy, but Jack put his hand up to stop them.

"Don't move, Maisy," he said quietly. "Rivermanders have bad senses out of water. It won't see you or smell you, unless you move."

Maisy stared down at the creature's outline as it slithered closer. She saw two red eyes on top of a big head, with purple, diamond-shaped irises. She wanted to run, but the monster's head rose out of the water. It looked like a giant salamander morphed with a great white shark. Maisy stared bug-eyed at three rows of sharp teeth. *Why don't I ever listen?* she thought.

"Why doesn't she ever listen?" Katy whispered.

The monster rose out of the water. It stood six feet tall, had no arms, and walked on two thick legs. It took a huge step toward Maisy and stopped so close she could feel its breath on her face. Maisy held her own breath. *That thing could swallow me whole!*

The monster lifted its neck, looking around for movement of any kind. Maisy saw two additional eyes on the creature's neck, near the corners of its jaw. The purple irises moved from side to side.

The monster turned its huge head. Maisy stood as still as the trees around her. Her face grew red as a cherry. She couldn't hold her breath much longer.

Just in time, the creature sank back into the water.

Maisy watched its outline swim away and disappear. Gasping and laughing, she bolted for Jack and the girls.

Chapter 7. The Dark Forest

They walked farther into the forest. The woods were so quiet, the girls could hear their own heartbeats. No birds sang their sweet songs. It grew darker and darker, until Jack and the girls couldn't see more than a few yards ahead. When Lillian looked up, all she saw was shadow. No light filtered through the canopy above.

But as their eyes slowly adjusted, they saw soft phosphorescent shapes glimmering in the blackness. Gleaming vines hung from high branches, some ending in red, spiky pods that ebbed as soft as glow sticks. Clusters of luminous bushes pressed tightly around the base of each tree.

After their eyes adjusted a little more, they saw a bush dotted with fluffy, round, pink pods the size of golf balls; long, brown spikes stabbed through the centers.

Pentagon-shaped pods glimmered on several trees. They grew flat against the trunks and were so perfectly shaped they didn't look natural. A shiny green ring ran around their edges. Inside that was a pink ring, a purple ring and a blue ring, ending with a red center. Things that looked like cherry-sized, crimson pompoms hung on each corner.

Surrounded by phosphorescent pods of so many shapes, sizes, and colors, the girls felt like they were in Wonderland at night.

"It's so beautiful," said Lillian.

"Yeah, yeah," interrupted Maisy. "Where's the food?"

"Everywhere," said Jack. He pointed at the glimmering bulbs on the bushes. "These are all fruit."

Maisy stepped closer and examined the strange pods. "These things look loathsome. Is there anything else?"

"Not until we leave the forest."

"Are you trying to poison me? In our world we don't eat things that glow."

"Well," said Jack, "we're not in your world."

"Can you show us how to eat these?" asked Lillian.

"Sure." Jack walked over to a tree. With both hands, he pulled off a big pentagon-shaped pod. He broke it in half, and offered a chunk to Katy.

"No, thank you," said Katy politely.

Jack smiled at Katy, then offered the fruit to Lillian. She took it, holding it like a big slice of watermelon. Inside, the fruit was brown and flaky.

Jack took a bite.

Lillian hesitated. "Will I glow?" she asked.

Jack smiled. "I don't know. You're human, so you might glow for the rest of your life."

Lillian grinned and took a bite. It was crunchy like a cracker, and sweet as cake. She swallowed. "This is really good."

Maisy walked up to a tree and yanked off a pentagon. Without even breaking it in half, she took a huge bite. "This is delicious!" she mumbled through a mouthful of food.

Jack picked another pentagon, broke off half, and offered it to Katy. She nibbled on it, smiled, and took a bigger bite.

After everyone finished eating, Jack led them deeper into the forest.

Soon, everyone was hungry again. Lillian looked at her watch. It was 6:30 p.m.

"I'm starving," said Maisy. "I say we all go pick pentagon fruit and meet back here."

"OK," said Jack. "But let's stick together."

They walked to the closest tree and picked more fruit. Jack collected other pods from the bushes around the tree, including a purple, melon-sized fruit shaped like an octahedron. They dumped all the pods and bulbs into one big pile and sat in the dark around the glowing fruit.

"Jack," asked Lillian, taking a bite, "how did this world get here?"

"Well," said Jack, "it all started a long time ago when monsters lived where humans live today. The earth had no houses or buildings or anything people made. Earth was all trees and rivers and waterfalls and mountains and everything natural. Everything was the way it should be. Peaceful and happy. Monsters and animals still ate each other; that's how nature works. But there were no wars, or killing each other for no reason.

"Then humans evolved. At first, monsters and humans shared the world. But as humans continued to evolve, they made tools and weapons, and after a while they didn't want to share the world with monsters. They wanted it all for themselves."

"Wow," whispered Katy.

"Wow is right," said Maisy, completely absorbed in eating fruit. "This stuff is delicious!"

"The humans made more weapons," Jack continued. "The monsters didn't realize that the humans were planning to take over the world, until the humans started attacking. They killed a lot of monsters, and completely wiped out all of the basilisks, leviathans, and even the fierce cyclops. We'll never see those creatures again."

Lillian felt angry. Why would anyone want to kill these great creatures?

Maisy ate happily, unaware of the conversation.

"After that," Jack shrugged helplessly, "the humans declared war. They used spears and bows and arrows. The monsters only had teeth and claws for weapons. After years of fighting, the monsters were almost extinct. To survive, they decided to hide from the humans. So they made this place, little by little, using a special magic. The monsters migrated down here to escape. Some monsters, like hydras, refused to live in hiding and were hunted to extinction. After the war, the humans thought all the monsters were gone. They celebrated."

"Why didn't the monsters use their magic to fight back?" asked Lillian.

"It's not that kind of magic," said Jack. "Monsters use their magic to create. Not to kill."

He broke a piece of fruit in half and gave it to Katy. "Eventually, people forgot that monsters ever existed. They made myths about all these creatures and passed them down, generation to generation, until people forgot that the stories were true.

"Thousands of years later, a scientist found a hydra skull. But monster bones aren't made of the same minerals as human bones, bird bones, or dinosaur bones. So the scientist built a mineral detector to find more monster bones. That led him to the beach. He dug deep into the sand but couldn't reach our world. So he built a huge robot to dig deeper, and the robot broke through to the path between the worlds.

"The scientist thought Lanodeka was amazing. He wanted to tell people about it, but the monsters wouldn't let him. The scientist begged the monsters to allow him to live down here. The monsters gave their permission, but only if he used his robot to guard

Lanodeka. That's how much they distrusted humans. And I can't blame them. No offense."

"None taken," said Katy. For the first time in her life, she felt sad about being human.

Jack continued. "When the scientist died, the monsters put an energy source inside the robot. That was the Guardian that attacked us.

"After that, the sirens asked the monsters to make a secret way in and out of Lanodeka. So the monsters used their magic to make the jetty."

"Why?" asked Katy.

"Sirens like to visit the human world sometimes," said Jack.

"Wouldn't people notice a siren?" asked Lillian.

"Sirens can transform," said Jack. "The monsters used their magic to hide Lanodeka so no human could ever find it, not without help. Then the sirens made two medallions to get into our world. They gave one of the medallions to my mom, which she eventually gave to me. Somehow, Bluebell found the other one. That's why I led her down here. She had the medallion."

"The sirens said that *you* were a siren," said Katy. "Is that true?"

"I'm half siren," said Jack.

"Where is Bluebell now?" asked Lillian.

Jack sighed. "I don't know. But ever since I led Bluebell down here, the world has changed. That's why I was sent to find you. We need your help."

Everyone sat silently as they ate their fruit, thinking

about all the things they had heard.

Noticing the silence, Maisy looked up from her food. "You know, Jack, you should tell us about this place sometime. I bet this world has a cool history."

They all laughed.

"What's so funny?" demanded Maisy.

Chapter 8. The Woman in the Tree

After following Jack for several hours, Lillian, Maisy, and Katy noticed that the forest was growing lighter.

"Are we almost through the woods?" asked Lillian.

"About a third of the way," said Jack.

"Is there a short cut?" complained Maisy.

"Actually," said Lillian, "if it only took us one day to get this far, in two more days we'll be out."

"I miss my parents," said Katy.

Fruit they hadn't seen before hung in the trees, and fallen fruit lay on the ground, still glowing.

As the forest grew steadily lighter, they saw small trees that were only a little taller than the girls themselves. These trees had tiny flowers that bloomed white, pink, blue, purple, yellow, red, and orange. Each of the flowers had four little petals.

The forest didn't feel so scary anymore.

Something moved just ahead of them. Everyone stopped and stared.

A woman seemed to walk right out of a tree. Instead of hair, she had long vines covered with leaves. Her skin was blue-green, and her bright green eyes were rimmed with light brown around black irises. She wore a dress made out of small white flowers.

"Hello," said the woman in a lilting voice, "I'm Anemone, a dryad. Who are you?"

The girls stared at this creature who looked like she could be Mother Nature herself.

"I'm Lillian. This is Katy, Maisy, and Jack."

Anemone looked them over. Her eyes lingered on Jack, sensing that he was more than human.

"I'm looking for my sister," said Lillian. "Can you help us find her? She has curly red hair—"

"Bluebell?" interrupted the dryad. A light breeze rustled her hair. "She came here about two years ago. Yesterday, she heard that *you* were in the world. She tried to find you but couldn't. So she went home, thinking that's where you were. You should go home too. Bluebell's waiting for you."

Anemone took a step toward Lillian. Leaning close, she whispered, "Besides, this world is too dangerous for someone like you."

Then Anemone stretched her arms out wide. Everyone watched as roots slowly rose out of the ground and twisted up around her legs, her waist, her arms, her head, until they couldn't see Anemone at all. In her place stood a small tree with green leaves and white flowers.

"Dryads used to tell the truth all the time," said Jack. "But now it's as if they're following someone else's orders. It's hard to know when they're lying."

Lillian crossed her arms. "But Anemone knew that Bluebell came here two years ago. She knew who Bluebell was. She sounded like she was telling the truth."

"If you leave," said Jack, "you'll get home and Bluebell won't be there."

"But I want to go home," whispered Katy.

"I want to stay," said Maisy.

"Why would Anemone lie?" asked Lillian. She looked at each one of them. Maisy smiled. Katy looked overwhelmed and scared. Jack looked confident. *Is Jack right? Is Anemone lying?*

"I need time to think," said Lillian. "By myself."

"Don't go too far," said Jack.

Lillian walked behind a big tree a few yards away. She looked around, alone for the first time in the forest. Spiky pods hung in the gloomy light high above, like the heads of monsters. Everything felt creepier now that she was alone.

Lillian sat, legs crossed, hands in her lap. The forest was as quiet as a photograph. Nothing moved. Only a little light filtered down from the trees above. The fruit around her shone dimly.

She stared at her right wrist. She still wore the friendship bracelet that Bluebell had made her a long time ago. Small wooden beads were threaded on either side of a wooden butterfly that was bright green when Lillian first wore it. Now the beads were dirty and the paint was peeling.

She remembered Bluebell at the County Fair. Lillian was seven or eight. They had saved up to buy carnival wristbands so they could go on any ride, all day. Bluebell didn't invite anyone, and neither did Lillian. It was just them. Sisters. Bluebell had convinced Lillian to go on her favorite ride, Mega Drop. Over-the-shoulder restraints locked Lillian into a foam rubber seat. That made her feel safe. After everyone was secure, the ride slowly rose higher and higher, 125 feet straight up. *What am I doing?* thought Lillian. The fair spread out below her. She saw the Ferris wheel in the distance slowly turning. When Mega Drop finally fell, Lillian actually rose six inches off her seat. The only thing that stopped her from flying away was the shoulder restraint which she clutched in terror. The wind whipped through her hair. She never knew anything could move that fast. The entire experience made her never want to go on a fast ride again. Bluebell felt bad that Lillian came off crying, so for the rest of the day she let Lillian pick all the rides.

Lillian looked up. She saw twisted branches covered with leaves, and remembered when Bluebell taught her how to climb out her bedroom window into the mulberry tree. Lillian was only four or five. Bluebell stepped on the window sill, walked onto the gable roof, grabbed one of the branches and pulled herself into the tree. Then Lillian stood on the edge of the window and leaned forward, but she was too short to reach the roof. Bluebell hung onto a branch and swung back into Lillian's bedroom. She grabbed a pink jump rope, handed it to Lillian, and climbed back into the tree. Bluebell reached out her hand. "Give me the rope." Lillian tossed the rope into the tree. Bluebell double knotted each end to a branch so the middle of the rope hung down. She climbed back into the room, grabbed a pillow, and draped the pillow over the bottom of the rope. She held both ends of the rope, sat on the pillow, and swung across. She used her feet to stop herself from slamming into the trunk. Then she lifted herself up, stood on the pillow, and climbed into the tree. "Now you try," she said. Lillian shook her head. "It's easy," said Bluebell as she climbed back into the room. She again grabbed both ends of the rope and sat on the pillow. Lillian slowly walked closer. "Sit on my lap," said Bluebell. "We'll do it together." Lillian carefully sat on her sister's lap and clutched the rope. Bluebell lifted her feet and they swung across the gap. Lillian slowly stood up on Bluebell's thighs and pulled herself into the tree. Bluebell clapped. "See, it wasn't that hard!" Bluebell climbed into the tree and found the V-shaped branch where she liked to sit. After that day, Lillian and Bluebell climbed the mulberry tree all the time, talking, reading and eating sweet mulberries. When they were up in those high branches, they always got along.

Lillian wished she had done more with Bluebell. *Would she leave this strange world just to find me? She might have once, but not anymore. I don't know what happened to our relationship, but she wouldn't come back for me now. She must still be here, and I can't leave without her.*

Lillian stood up. The forest looked a little brighter. The fruit seemed more radiant. Bluebell was here somewhere and Lillian was going to find her.

She pulled at a huge, colorful pentagon. Snap! The fruit popped off the tree. Crunch! Lillian broke it in half and took a bite. The fruit tasted better than anything she had eaten in her entire life.

Lillian walked back into the clearing. Maisy and Katy saw in Lillian's face that they were going to stay.

Maisy smiled. "Yes!" She did a victory dance.

Katy sighed. *I guess there's nothing else to do. If we turn back now, it'll break Lillian's heart.*

"You made the right decision," said Jack.

"If I had decided to leave, would you let us go?" asked Lillian.

Once again, Jack didn't answer.

"In other words," said Maisy, "you made the *only* decision."

Chapter 9. More Than a Lion

The forest became darker again as Jack and the girls walked. After an hour or so, the pentagon-shaped fruit were all gone, along with the rest of the fruit they had seen earlier, and new kinds of fruit glowed on the trees. Lillian noticed an azure fruit with green stripes across smooth skin; violet dots circled between the stripes.

The only sound was the leaves crunching under their feet.

Then they heard a new noise, a *buzzzzzzz*, like hundreds of bees flying above them.

The girls looked up and saw small creatures swarming in the dim air. They shone bright yellow like hummingbird-sized lanterns.

"What are they?" Lillian asked in awe.

"Pixies," said Jack.

The pixies flew closer. They didn't have legs or feet. Instead, they had tails that flapped up and down as they buzzed toward the girls. Their tails looked like triangles of glowing yellow skin, stretched across two minuscule bones.

The girls stared. This was one of the most amazing things they had ever seen.

The pixies hovered closer. Their small three-fingered hands ended in talons. They had sharp, white teeth and pink eyes with large, dark blue pupils.

Katy took a step back. "Jack, are they safe?"

"They only look mean to scare off predators," he said.

Maisy reached out and tried to grab a pixie, but it danced away.

The pixies whirred all around the girls, grabbing their hair, hovering right in front of their noses, making faces, and sticking out tiny tongues. Jack swatted at any pixie that came too close to him.

"Don't you like pixies?" asked Lillian. She smoothed her hair, forcing the pixies to let go.

"They're annoying," said Jack.

Katy tried to keep the pixies away but they wouldn't leave her alone. They zipped around her, pulling on her hair and clothes.

Maisy stuck her tongue out at the pixies. "Jack has a point. Stop pulling my hair!"

All of the pixies laughed, sounding like hundreds of tiny violins playing very high notes.

Maisy snatched wildly at the pixies, jumping and

cursing, waving her arms, chasing them one way then the other. "Stupid, brainless creatures!"

"Maisy, stop," said Lillian.

"Leave me alone, you nasty mosquitoes!"

Suddenly the pixies flew away into the treetops. They entered the canopy of leaves, disappearing like little candles blown out by the wind.

"That's right!" yelled Maisy. "You better run! Thou art as loathsome as toads!"

"There she goes with the Shakespearean insults," Katy whispered to Lillian.

"Who knew that being forced to read *Titus Andronicus* could be so useful?" said Maisy.

"It's almost impossible to scare a pixie," said Jack.

"Oh, yeah!" Maisy did a victory dance. "I scared off something that's impossible to scare off!"

Jack scanned the area. "No. It was something much more dangerous than you."

He stared at a huge bush. The girls followed his gaze, but didn't see or hear anything.

Jack took a step back. "Something's there." The bushes shook. The girls took a step back too.

A large lion exploded out of the bushes with a rumbling roar that shook the forest. Katy screamed as Lillian and Maisy stumbled back in surprise.

The lion crouched and stared hungrily at them. Now the girls saw a goat's head attached to its back. Then the tail came up from behind, but instead of a tail it was a snake at least nine feet long, green and thick as a boa constrictor. The creature towered over them, bigger than an elephant.

"Chimera," Jack whispered.

They felt their hearts pounding in their chests. Without thinking, they all bolted in different directions. Jack grabbed Katy's hand and pulled her after him. The chimera charged right at Lillian, hurtling over bushes and crashing through the underbrush. Lillian heard the deep roar behind her and ran faster, gasping, dodging between trees.

"Over here!" Jack sounded far away.

The chimera skidded to a stop and turned around.

Jack put his first and second fingers into his mouth and whistled.

The chimera hesitated, looking from Lillian to Jack. Then it turned and ran after Jack.

Now that Jack and Katy weren't in a clearing, they could only see the outline of the chimera in the dark forest. But when it passed a glowing fruit, they caught glimpses of a lion's fierce face or a snake's sharp fangs.

Jack yanked Katy's hand and they sprinted through the trees. He pulled Katy between two trunks that grew close together.

"What were you thinking?!" shouted Katy. "We don't want the chimera to follow us!"

"Lillian can't outrun a chimera," said Jack.

"Neither can we!" said Katy.

The chimera roared behind them.

Jack steered Katy around the tight trees. Katy heard splintering and snapping as the chimera tore through the trunks and came running after them. She tried not to think about what would happen if the chimera caught them. *Me and Jack are the main meal, Maisy is the side dish, and Lillian will be dessert!*

Lillian ran through the dark forest. *The chimera must be right behind me,* she thought. But she didn't hear it anymore.

She stopped, still breathing hard, and looked around. *Where are Jack, Katy, and Maisy? I wish I had believed the dryad. Now I'm lost in the forest! The chimera must have gone after Jack. He probably died to save us.*

Lillian sat on a tree stump. She peered into the shadows and listened. Because it was so dark, she couldn't even see the trees. The eerie light of the fruit seemed to float in the air all around her. Nothing moved. Nothing looked beautiful anymore. It only looked haunted.

I should keep going, she thought. *But I don't know if I'm moving backwards or forwards. And if chimeras live here, then who knows what other kinds of monsters live here too. But if I don't keep moving, I'll never see my family, friends, or anyone again. What will mom and dad think when they find I'm gone? I disappeared as mysteriously as Bluebell.*

Lillian took a deep breath. She knelt, took off her backpack, and opened it. She groped around until she felt the cold metal of her flashlight. She stood and clicked on the light. "OK. Let's go."

Maisy ran through the forest, then stopped. The chimera wasn't following her.

"Jack, why didn't we hear the chimera sneak up on us?" said Maisy. "Uh ... Jack, you still here? Lillian? Katy? Is *anyone* here?"

Maisy listened but only heard her voice echo faintly in the dark. "Jack! Lillian! Katy!" She wandered deeper into the forest, shouting their names.

"They should have followed me," she muttered. "Or at least let me know where they were going. But no, they just ran off in different directions!"

She bent down and unzipped her backpack. "Those blockheads. Jack was the one who was so worried about splitting up. Now he runs off to save himself!"

She threw things carelessly out of her backpack until she found the flashlight. "I have to do everything myself. As usual."

Jack and Katy ran as fast as they could, panting, their hearts pounding as the chimera crashed through the bushes behind them. Katy winced at the splintering of trunks being torn apart. She looked behind her.

Jack yanked on her hand. "Keep moving!"

Katy ran faster but fell behind because she kept looking over her shoulder. The chimera was only an outline in the dark, then suddenly it passed a glowing fruit and Katy caught glimpses of the lion.

"Don't look back!" shouted Jack. Katy ran faster than she had ever run in her life.

The chimera roared. Katy cringed. She felt the sound shake through her body.

Jack led Katy through narrow gaps between the trees. The chimera's claws ripped the trunks apart. A storm of leaves tumbled through the air. Katy held her free arm over her head to block the leaves.

Thud! The chimera tore through a thick tree. It shook the ground. Katy stumbled. Jack pulled her up. The chimera roared, more angry than before. Whatever a chimera chases, it catches, and it wasn't going to let Jack and Katy get away. It tore through the wood using claws and teeth.

We're going to die! thought Katy.

Chapter 10. Lost

Lillian moved her flashlight from side to side. The dim, hazy circle of light made the forest look different. The geometric fruit stopped glowing when she passed the light over it, appearing mechanical rather than magical.

She saw something shiny to the right. As she turned the flashlight, a unicorn stepped out from behind a tree. It had a creamy white horn at least three feet long, and a mane and tail of the same color. Its body glimmered.

Lillian stared, transfixed, then slowly bent and put her flashlight on the ground. She reached out one hand and took a step toward the unicorn. A little groove corkscrewed all the way up to the tip of the horn. It looked like someone had taken a brush and painted the inside of the groove with abalone blue.

Lillian stopped moving. She felt wonder fill her

body like a big breath of air. She stared at the unicorn, and the unicorn stared at her. The whites of its eyes were as pure as a calla lily, and its pupils were as beautiful as black Tahitian pearls. *Who would kill these amazing creatures?* she thought. *But even in our world we kill the most amazing animals, like deer, sea turtles, wolves, tigers, and whales. People seem to have no respect or compassion for the animals that they kill, eat, wear, and capture for their own amusement.*

She took one step closer and stretched out her hand, her fingers only inches away from the unicorn. Lillian felt the warmth coming off the unicorn's body. She leaned forward … but the unicorn's eyes widened, its ears lifted, and it galloped away.

Lillian's hand still hovered over the spot where the unicorn had been. She sighed. *Why did I think that a unicorn would let me touch it?*

Suddenly, the chimera roared far off in the dark. Lillian picked up her flashlight and ran toward the sound. *The chimera just caught one of my friends!*

Then Lillian heard something else. She stopped running and listened. At first, all she could hear was her own raspy breath. Then came a familiar voice:

"Lillian! Jack! Katy!"

A surge of hope rushed through Lillian's body. "Maisy!" She turned and ran toward her friend's voice.

Jack tugged hard on Katy's hand. She ran as fast as she could, but she had been running so long she had a stitch in her side. The chimera was close behind them, snapping at the backs of their heads.

"Faster!" Jack yelled.

Katy heard a roar. She jumped and ran faster.

Jack pulled Katy to the right.

"What are you doing?!" yelled Katy.

Jack pointed to a dark seam in the bottom of a tree. He quickly pushed Katy into the hole, then ducked inside. Katy looked up. She saw that the entire tree was hollowed out like a wooden tube. The roots of the fruit hanging on the outside of the trunk glimmered faintly on the inside, like colorful spiderwebs. The light revealed branches growing *inside* the tree, in every direction, all the way to the top.

"Wow," breathed Katy.

Jack pushed her up onto the lowest branch. "Go!"

Katy scrabbled up, and Jack quickly climbed after her. There was lots of room inside the big tree. Katy had never climbed a tree before, and slipped on some of the branches. Jack was right behind her, urging her to go faster.

The tree shook as huge claws ripped through the trunk and shredded the branch under Jack's feet. Katy gasped and stopped climbing. She looked down to see Jack grip the branch above and pull himself onto it. When Katy saw the splintered tear in the trunk and heard the chimera sniffing at the hole, she realized that the tree she thought was safe was actually more dangerous than running through the forest.

Crash! The chimera's long, sharp claws tore through the tree only inches from Jack. *It's climbing the tree!*

Katy made a little squeak of fear as she watched from a wobbling branch. Jack put a finger to his lips, then pointed upward. But Katy just stood on the branch, paralyzed.

Move! Jack mouthed to her, but she couldn't. She heard the chimera sniffing through the holes it had just slashed in the trunk. Its big, black nose pressed against the slits in the tree, smelling the air. Then it huffed a huge breath that almost knocked Jack off his branch. The stink of rotten flesh filled the tree.

That sickening stench made Katy realize she was only meat to the chimera. She started climbing again, bumping her knees and scuffing her elbows, her heart pounding until all she could hear was her own breath.

Jack stepped on one of the branches. Snap! He fell until he grabbed another branch and quickly climbed after Katy.

Claws slashed through the bark, barely missing Katy's face. She closed her eyes as dust and splinters flew, stinging her cheeks. She gasped and opened her eyes. She heard the chimera right outside the tree, sniffing for her. Terror rose inside her like cold water.

The chimera glared through the holes. Its narrowed eyes scanned inside, then fixed on Katy. She bolted higher into the tree. Jack followed, right behind her.

The chimera tore a big hole, pulled through the breach, and heaved itself into the tree. It looked up and saw a maze of branches growing from the tree wall into the center. Jack and Katy climbed above. The chimera growled as it pushed itself through the tight spaces.

Jack and Katy stopped climbing and looked down. Katy screamed when she saw the chimera *inside* the tree. She quickly started to climb again. She scuffed her elbows, ripped her jeans, and bruised her knees. Jack climbed right behind her.

Katy heard the chimera gaining on them. Every time it roared it sounded closer.

She looked up. The inside of the tree narrowed as they climbed higher, and the branches grew thinner and further apart. She grabbed another branch. Snap!

She looked down at Jack. "We're trapped! The branches are too small!"

Jack turned and watched the chimera below. It used the bigger branches to climb, and snapped the smaller branches out of its way.

Then, as the chimera squeezed through two thick branches, its shoulders got stuck. It growled as it tried to break free.

"Katy," said Jack, "this is our chance."

"What do you mean?"

"We need to climb back down."

Katy stared at Jack. "You want me to climb past the chimera?!"

"We're dinner if we stay here," said Jack.

He climbed down a few branches, then stopped and looked up at Katy. Reluctantly, she followed.

"I wish I was home," Katy whimpered. "This is my last day on earth and I'm spending it in a tree!"

The chimera's growls turned into roars as they climbed closer. Its muscles bulged under its dirty fur, and its mane was tangled with twigs. The chimera looked like it could break out of the branches any second. The snake tail swayed, waiting for them to come within reach, its yellow eyes shifting between Jack and Katy. Its thin, emotionless pupils made its eyes more horrifying than the lion's.

Katy watched Jack squeeze through the branches. The chimera swiped at him, but couldn't reach. Katy stood on a branch above, frozen with fear, which turned into dread when she heard *Hiss …*

She slowly raised her head. The snake at the end of the chimera's tail hovered in front of her. Suddenly, it lunged at Katy's face. Long, sharp fangs snapped so close to her nose that cold saliva sprayed her cheeks.

"Yuck!" Katy yelped as she quickly followed Jack past the chimera. The lion growled, its eyes staring wildly at her, paws swiping, claws gouging the big branches that trapped it.

The smell of rotten meat made Katy feel sick. She stared right into the snarling mouth. The sharp teeth looked like small knives.

Jack stopped to let Katy pass, then they both scrambled down as fast as they could go. They heard the chimera roaring above. Little pieces of wood fell on their heads as the chimera struggled to get free.

Katy heard a loud crack, followed by a roar that echoed through the tree. The chimera broke loose, whipped around, and plunged headfirst down the tree.

Snap! The chimera broke more branches, struggling to keep its balance, climbing after Jack and Katy.

Jack jumped and landed by the opening. Katy climbed down the last few branches, then hopped to the ground. They both ducked out of the tree just as the chimera leapt and burst through the seam.

Crash! Wood flew all around them. Jack and Katy tripped and fell on the ground. They rolled over and found the chimera standing above them, one massive paw on either side. It growled hungrily and leaned toward Katy. She threw her hands in front of her face. The chimera opened its mouth. Katy smelled rotten meat again.

I'm going to die, she thought. *I'm really going to die!*

Katy waited to feel sharp teeth sink into her skin. Instead, she heard the chimera growl deep in its chest. It almost sounded scared. Katy uncovered her eyes. The chimera stared over their heads as it slowly backed away.

Katy rolled onto her stomach to see what the chimera was staring at—and saw a beautiful white unicorn step out from between the trees.

For a moment, Katy just stared in awe at the unicorn. It galloped forward, then jumped over them and charged the chimera.

The chimera roared and swiped at the unicorn with its big claws. The unicorn dodged out of reach, then reared and kicked the chimera's face with its front hooves. The chimera roared in pain and stumbled back.

As the mythical creatures fought, Jack saw something out of the corner of his eye: a pack of wood elves, bone white, watching from the gloom of the trees.

Katy saw them too. *Ghosts!* she thought.

Jack sprang up and extended his hand to Katy. She took it. He pulled her up and led her toward the elves.

"What are you doing?!" shouted Katy.

As Katy drew closer to the creatures, she saw that they weren't ghosts at all. They looked like skeletons with thin, transparent skin stretched across their small, gaunt bodies. They were so pale, as if they had never seen sunlight. She closed her eyes seconds before Jack pulled her into the pack of ghastly creatures.

The chimera's snake tail jabbed at the unicorn, who slapped the snake with its horn.

Suddenly, the unicorn and the chimera stopped fighting and looked to the right. The pack of wood elves ran toward them, shaking spears and waving nets in the air. The elves wailed and howled.

The unicorn galloped away. But before the chimera could escape, the elves threw a net and drew it down tight. The chimera struggled, roared, and snapped its powerful jaws. But there were too many wood elves, and the chimera couldn't tear the net. The chimera thrust its tail through the holes in the net, but the elves were too far away for the snake to reach. More elves ran up and hammered wood stakes into the ground, securing the net.

Katy opened her eyes. Some of the wood elves walked toward her. They were about two feet tall and white as ash. *These creatures aren't so scary,* she thought.

But as they came closer, she saw that they were just skin and bone, without any muscles or tendons or hair at all. They looked like living skeletons. One of the elves stared up at her. She stepped back in shock: the small creature didn't have eyes or a nose. Instead, translucent skin stretched over its eye sockets and nasal cavity.

They all gathered around Katy. She looked for an opening in the ring of elves, but she was surrounded. The elves held knives, spears, sacks, and nets.

She turned to Jack. "What are these things?"

"Wood elves," said Jack. "I usually get along fine with them, but they're upset about something."

Katy stepped through the elves. "They don't look like Orlando Bloom." They all turned to watch her.

She looked around and saw the chimera in the net.

"Thank you for saving us," she said to the elves, who just stared up her. "Jack, are they herbivores?"

"No," he said, "but usually they don't eat anything larger than themselves."

"Usually?" squeaked Katy.

Two elves snuck up behind Katy and Jack, jumped, and threw one big sack over them. More elves pulled the sack down. Jack and Katy fell hard.

"Ow!" shouted Katy. "Jack, what's happening?!"

It was even darker in the sack than in the forest. Katy could only see the outline of Jack's face as the elves dragged them over stones, through bushes, and even bumped them off of tree trunks.

"Ow!" yipped Katy. "I thought you said — ow! that wood elves usually — ow! don't go — ow! after anything bigger than — ow! themselves!"

"Like I said," Jack sighed, "things have changed."

The elves dragged the sack deeper into the forest.

Chapter 11. The White Elves

Maisy stopped running, bent over with her hands on her knees, and listened. She didn't hear the chimera. She didn't hear anything but her own panting breath.

She clicked off her flashlight. The forest was so dark she couldn't even see the ground. Out in the blackness, little stars glowed, a spattering of reds, greens, and blue-violets. She knew those tiny lights were actually fruit.

Great. I'm lost. I wouldn't be lost if those dumbos had followed me. I started running first, so they should have followed ME! Then Jack would be here to lead us out! I can't believe those blockheads!

"Lillian! Jack! Katy!" she called again, then listened. "Lillian?! Jack?! Katy?!"

The silence seemed to be saying: *You're lost!*

"Great, I'm spending the rest of my life in this stupid, miserable, dark forest!"

She took off her backpack and unzipped the front. She reached inside, muttering to herself. "Now my backpack is almost empty because of Lillian. Taking other people's food. The little thief."

She clicked on her flashlight again, and shone the light into the murky darkness. The beam of white moved from side to side and up and down, but didn't reveal anything except trees and bushes.

"Those half-wits," mumbled Maisy.

She walked up to a bush and picked a piece of fruit. It was round, purple, and squishy. She sat down, put her flashlight in her lap, and held the fruit in one hand. "Can you believe my friends left me?" she complained to the fruit. "Can you believe I'm talking to a piece of fruit?"

She took a huge bite and felt like she had bitten into a soggy sponge. The fruit was pink inside and tasted like a rotten tomato.

Maisy threw it into the darkness. "Disgusting!"

She stood up, walked over to a tree and picked a different fruit: it was aquamarine and as long as a rolling pin. It had red stripes on the sides.

She grumbled at an imaginary Lillian, Jack, and Katy. "I scorn you, scurvy companions." She took a bite. The fruit was crunchy like an apple, but tasted like a banana. "What, you poor, base, rascally, cheating, lack-linen mates!" Maisy took another bite. "Away, you moldy rogues, away."

Whenever she was assigned Shakespeare, Maisy always flipped through the pages until she found an insult, which she memorized. She had dozens of Shakespearean insults down pat. But for the first time, they didn't make her feel better.

I'm lost. Probably forever. I should have stayed with Jack, Katy, and Lillian. Why do I alway act before I think? I always do things without considering the consequences. Lillian always thinks things through for us, so I never do. I have to stop being so careless. I need to act more mature. I need to be more like Lillian. Not that I'd tell her that.

Maisy stood up. "Lillian! Jack! Katy!" She wandered farther into the forest, shouting as she went.

Lillian sped toward Maisy's voice. The dim beam of her flashlight bobbed up and down as she ran. She saw the rough bark of the trunks with moss growing in the cracks. Bushes glowed with colorful fruit, but the fruit stopped glowing when hit by the flashlight.

Maisy's voice sounded closer. "Lillian! Jack! Katy!"

Lillian felt hope rise inside her. Then she saw something that turned her hope into dread. Twenty yards to her right, a pack of small, white creatures were also running toward Maisy's voice. They had big heads compared to their tiny bodies. Their skin was as white as sheets and as transparent as tracing paper. They didn't see Lillian.

She ran faster, but the creatures were too quick. Lillian fell behind.

I have to get to Maisy before they do! she thought. *Should I call out to warn her? But I don't want them coming after me.*

In a clearing up ahead, she saw Maisy surrounded by the pale creatures. Lillian bent down, picked up a stone and hid behind a tree, waiting to see what would happen.

Jack's and Katy's eyes adjusted to the darkness in the sack. They both sat on their rears now, but the ride was still bumpy and painful. Jack pulled apart a few threads in the woven sack. All he could see was the sylvan darkness strung with gleaming fruit: scarlet, jade, ultramarine, and primrose gold. It looked beautiful.

Katy tried to stay calm, but she couldn't. She kept looking around and biting her nails, whimpering whenever they hit a rock.

"What's your favorite movie?" Jack asked, trying to distract her.

"*The Princess Bride, Nightmare Before Christmas, Titanic*—" Katy mumbled.

"Pick one," said Jack.

Katy didn't answer. *What are these creatures going to do with us?*

"Tell me about *The Princess Bride*," said Jack.

Are they going to eat us? Are they—

"Tell me about *The Princess Bride*," said Jack, gently tapping her shoulder.

"What?" said Katy.

"*The Princess Bride.*"

"Oh." Katy just stared at Jack as they were dragged over a rock. "Ouch! Well, the main characters got stuck in a forest too. They were almost killed by the R.O.U.S., Rodents of Unusual Size—"

"Tell me about *Titanic.*"

"There's a character named Jack, like you, but he dies, like we're probably—"

"Tell me about *Nightmare Before Christmas.*"

"There's another character named Jack. He's a skeleton, so he'd feel right at home here with these bony carnivores who are probably going to—Ouch!"

Suddenly, they were being dragged over bumpier ground. Jack pulled on a few threads of the sack. He saw a dry riverbed. The rocks were gray and black. The stones glimmered like the fruit with a faint light.

"Ouch!" yelped Katy.

The ground became smooth again.

Katy looked even more worried.

"What do you like to do?" said Jack.

"Why are you asking me about movies and hobbies at a time like this?!"

Jack touched Katy on her knee. "Is there anything we can do right now?"

Katy hesitated. "No."

"Can we get out of this sack?"

"No."

"Will worrying make you feel better or worse?"

Katy didn't answer.

"Better or worse?"

Katy looked away. "Worse."

"I'm trying to distract you, so you won't have to worry until there's something we can do."

Katy didn't say anything at first. "Well, I play harp, violin, and clarinet. I take archery lessons, I like to write in my journal, do origami—"

"Archery?" Jack asked in surprise. "How long have you been taking archery?"

"Seven years. I took classes with Lillian and Maisy when we were little."

"Are they any good at it?"

"Maisy quit halfway through the first class, and Lillian quit after the fifth."

"Why did you keep going?"

"My grandma took me. We went together every week. When I went to her house, we'd practice in her backyard. Now I have a target in my own backyard. I use her bow from the Olympics. She won gold medals long before I was even born. A Celtic knot design is engraved all the way up my grandma's bow. I'd press my thumb on the pattern until it marked my skin like an ornamental blister. She always made lemonade. When we took breaks from practicing, she'd tell me I'd go to the Olympics someday too. A year ago, my grandma died. I inherited her bow. It's the most important thing I own."

"Do you want to go to the Olympics?"

Katy nodded. "But don't tell anyone. It's a secret."

As they talked, the elves dragged them deeper into the heart of the starless forest.

"Get away, you idiots!"

The creatures stood around Maisy in an uneven circle, pointing short spears at her. She passed her flashlight over their faces. They looked like skeletons with transparent skin.

The creatures didn't like the light. Some of them jumped up and grabbed at it. Maisy held her flashlight up out of reach.

"Hey! This is mine!"

One of the wood elves jumped and snatched the light out of Maisy's hand.

"Give me that!" she shouted.

The elves pounced on the flashlight as if it was some kind of small animal they could eat. They stabbed at it with their spears.

"Hey!" shouted Maisy. "Stop that!"

The flashlight bounced up and down as the elves stabbed at it. Light flared on the forest floor, the leaves above, the tree trunks, and Maisy's angry face. An elf thrust its spear and whack! the light went out, leaving the forest in sudden darkness.

Lillian, still hiding behind the tree, couldn't see anything. There was a moment of horrible silence, broken by Maisy's cursing. Then Maisy's voice sounded muffled and farther away.

Lillian felt her heart pounding. As her eyes

adjusted again to the dark, she saw the clearing, barely illuminated by glowing fruit.

Maisy was gone.

Lillian stepped out from behind the tree and looked around. For one terrifying moment, she thought something had happened to Maisy. *Did the creatures hurt her? Did they kill her?*

Then she heard Maisy's muffled cursing. Lillian spun around. Fifty yards ahead, she saw the wood elves dragging a large sack into the dark. Lillian chased after the elves but immediately tripped over a big root.

"Ow!" she gasped before she could stop herself. Luckily, she was too far behind for the creatures to hear. She rubbed her toes through her shoes, got back up and ran again, but this time bumped her knee on a tree stump. She bit her lip to stop herself from crying out. Massaging her knee, she watched the white creatures growing smaller and smaller.

She quickly got up and ran through the inky forest. But after stumbling over rocks and tripping over roots and scraping her knees and elbows, she stopped and looked at her flashlight. *If I turn it on, the creatures might see me. If I don't, I can't help Maisy.*

She clicked on her flashlight and pointed it down. The beam illuminated the bumpy earth. Avoiding rocks and roots, she sprinted toward the faint sound of Maisy's cursing.

One of the creatures stopped and tilted its

cadaverous head, listening. Lillian quickly hid behind a tree and clicked off her flashlight.

The elves whipped around and scanned the area. They pointed their spears at the tree Lillian was hiding behind. Their footsteps grew louder as they came closer. Scratch! A spear scraped against the bark of the tree. Lillian didn't move.

Then she saw something white running right at her. As it came closer, she recognized the unicorn. She felt her fear melt. Lillian stretched out her hand, hoping to touch it, but the unicorn galloped by.

She heard the wood elves yelling in their flat, nasally voices. Their feet scrambled through the underbrush.

The tree Lillian stood behind was so big she had to take a step to the side to look around it. Most of the elves were running after the unicorn. But in a moment, the unicorn had disappeared into the darkness.

The wood elves reformed their group and dragged the sack holding Maisy farther into the forest. Lillian waited a few seconds, just in case the elves looked over their shoulders, then turned on the flashlight and ran after them.

Lillian saw something far ahead. At first, it looked like a white blob in the dark. But as it drew closer, she saw that it was another pack of elves. This hunting party was bigger than the one Lillian was following. She hid behind a tree, turned off her flashlight and watched. These elves were also dragging a sack, bigger than the sack Maisy was in.

"Katy and Jack," whispered Lillian.

She watched as the groups met. The elves yelled and bickered over their sacks.

What am I going to do now? Lillian thought.

Chapter 12. The Fort in the Clearing

Jack and Katy heard the wood elves fighting.

"What are they saying?" asked Katy.

"I don't know," said Jack.

Then, over the sounds of the shouting and bickering, they heard a familiar voice.

"You walnut-brained, puny-boned, flat-faced shorties! Let me out or you won't live to regret it!"

"Maisy!" whispered Katy. "You know she's really mad when she forgets to use Shakespearean insults."

Jack laughed. "I wonder if Lillian is with her."

The top of their sack stretched open, then the elves pulled the rough cloth down around them. Compared to the pitch black inside the sack, the dark forest looked almost bright. Jack stood up and reached out to Katy. She took his hand and he pulled her up.

"You half-witted peewee thugs—!"

A small elf kicked Maisy.

"Ouch!"

"Maisy!" shouted Katy.

"Katy?!"

Elves yanked open the sack that held Maisy, grabbed the bottom, and wrenched it up over their heads. Maisy tumbled out and rolled like a potato to Katy's feet.

Maisy looked up. "Did they put you in a stupid sack too?"

"I'm so glad to see you!" exclaimed Katy.

Maisy stood up and brushed the dirt off her jeans. "Is Lillian with you? She has all my food."

Jack pointed at the wood elves. "We have more important things to worry about."

Thump! Katy whipped around and saw the wood elves chopping branches off the smaller trees.

"What are they doing?" she asked.

Jack looked worried. "I don't know. I haven't seen them do this before."

Maisy leaned toward Katy. "Do you have any *real* food?" she whispered out of the corner of her mouth.

Katy gazed at Maisy. *This is what I love and hate about you,* she thought. *You are always yourself. No matter where we are or what we're doing, you're always yourself. Even now, in a life-and-death situation, you're thinking about food. Sometimes that's annoying but that's you, and that's what I love about you, you loon.*

Katy threw her arms around Maisy.

Maisy patted her on the back with one hand. "It's OK, don't worry." But with her other hand, Maisy quietly unzipped Katy's backpack, reached in, groped around, found a granola bar, and slipped it out.

One elf grabbed Katy's shins, another grabbed Maisy's jeans. Gibbering in their high, nasally voices, they pulled the girls apart. Katy tripped backward and landed on her bottom. Jack reached out a hand and again helped Katy to her feet.

As Maisy stumbled backwards, an elf jumped and snatched the granola bar out of her hand.

"Hey! That's mine!" said Maisy.

Katy grinned. "I thought you said Lillian took all your food."

Whack! Elves struck Maisy and Katy behind the knees. The girls fell forward and their knees hit the ground hard. They cried out in pain as an elf swung his spear at Jack's legs, but Jack jumped over it. The elf shook its spear at Katy and yelled. Jack put his hands up and knelt on the ground.

Katy looked around at all the creatures. Even on her knees, she was taller than the elves. Some of them pointed their spears violently.

Suddenly, an elf jumped onto Jack's shoulder. Its feet had tiny claws on each toe that clung to Jack's shirt. Jack didn't move, but Katy flinched. The elf held a black piece of cloth, looped it over Jack's head, pulled it tight across his eyes, and tied the ends together. The cloth wasn't as rough as the sack, but it was still itchy.

"Why are they blindfolding us?" said Katy.

Maisy narrowed her eyes. "Don't you blockheads even *think* about blindfolding me."

An elf pounced onto Maisy's shoulder. It was smaller than the others, with smaller claws, so it grabbed Maisy's hair to keep its balance.

Whump! Maisy punched the wood elf off her shoulder. The small elf hit the ground with a thud.

Another elf held a spear to Maisy's throat. The same small elf jumped up onto her shoulder. This time, Maisy didn't move as the elf stretched the blindfold around her head and pulled the black cloth tighter than usual, chuckling as it tied the knot.

A big elf hopped onto Katy's shoulder. She felt like a deer pounced on by a leopard. Its sharp claws poked through her shirt. Katy whimpered, trying to stay calm as the blindfold made everything go black.

The elf's claws just ruined my shirt, thought Katy. *This was a good shirt! Why am I thinking about a shirt?!*

A pair of elves walked up to Maisy. One elf held three short pieces of rope while the other forced Maisy's hands together.

Maisy tried to wrench her hands free. "Get away from me!"

But the elf was so strong she couldn't budge. "You boneheads are tiny but mighty," Maisy grumbled. The other elf tied Maisy's wrists together.

The small creatures did the same to Jack and Katy. Then the elves pulled on the lengths of rope like they were leading dogs. Jack and the girls staggered blindly into the forest, their hands stretched in front of them.

Lillian clicked on her flashlight and prowled after them. *Like Theses,* she thought. *I wish I was as bold as Theses, king of Athens, slayer of the Minotaur. I might actually meet a Minotaur! Or worse, a sphinx. Who knows what lives in this forest?*

Up ahead, she saw the white pack of elves and the silhouettes of Jack, Maisy, and Katy. Jack seemed to turn his head in her direction, as if he knew she was there.

What does he expect me to do? I came here to find Bluebell, not to fight monsters! I wish we had turned around when we had the chance. I should have listened to mom and dad. It's all my fault. I shouldn't have forced Maisy and Katy to come. Now if they get hurt or killed, it'll be because of me.

Lillian followed the elves. The forest seemed scarier and darker than ever.

Lillian saw little bright green lights floating high in the distance. The lights passed behind trees as she walked, reappearing brighter and closer, flickering like flames hovering in the air. Under each light Lillian saw something that looked like a wooden pillar, about four feet wide and as tall as a three-story building. As she got closer, she saw that each pillar was a log that had been stripped of bark and branches, and sharpened at the end into a spike.

The trees thinned out as the forest opened into a huge, bright clearing. Now Lillian saw shorter pillars between the tall ones. These pillars were also stripped of bark and branches, and the ends had been sharpened to pointy tips. All of the logs stood so close together that a piece of paper couldn't fit between them. They made a wall so high Lillian could only see the tops of tall trees growing from the other side.

She clicked off her flashlight and hid behind the last tree at the edge of the clearing. She watched the elves lead Jack, Maisy, and Katy toward the pale brown wall.

The elf in the lead reached into a pocket and pulled out a rough, rectangular rock. The elf walked up to the gate and tapped the rock against one pillar and then another. Lillian watched as the two pillars sprang up seven feet in the air. Jack, Maisy, and Katy were led through the opening, followed by all the other elves. As soon as they were through, the two logs fell back down with a mighty thud.

Lillian stared at the wall, then looked around. After she made sure no wood elves were still outside, she quickly ran across the clearing. She bent down, picked up a rock and tapped the same logs that the elf had tapped, but nothing happened.

Jack, Katy, and Maisy heard hundreds of elves yelling, and the patter of their clawed feet all around. Some elves had higher voices and others had lower voices, but all of the voices were loud and nasally. They sounded like a band of out-of-tune kazoos.

The elves took the prisoners' blindfolds off, but kept their hands tied. The light dazzled Jack, Katy, and Maisy; they hadn't seen this much light since they entered the forest.

The girls looked around in amazement and fear. Inside the fort, hundreds of wood elves milled about. They sharpened spears and knives, wove fabrics for sacks and clothes, whittled cages, and tied strings into nets. Smaller elves ran around yelling and bickering. All the elves stopped what they were doing and looked at the new arrivals.

"An elf village," whispered Katy.

"More like a skeleton village," muttered Maisy.

They looked up and saw houses in the trees. Some were bigger than others, but even the biggest ones were only the size of a one-room cabin. The houses looked like they were made out of Lincoln Logs but with flat roofs. They saw a bunch of elves quickly scaling up and down ladders to the houses. The ladders were little more than pieces of wood tied together by lengths of thin, frayed rope.

"The houses have no windows," said Katy.

"Wood elves don't like windows," said Jack.

Katy stared at the big wall that surrounded them, dotted by the bright flames. There was no way out.

The elves tugged on their ropes, but this time led Katy and Maisy one way, and Jack another.

"There separating us!" said Katy.

"Don't resist right now," warned Jack, "or they might do something even worse."

The elves led Katy and Maisy to a rickety rope ladder. An elf grabbed a small knife out of its belt and cut the bonds tying their hands together. Other elves yanked off their backpacks. Then one elf began to climb. It glanced over its shoulder and motioned for the girls to follow.

"This'll be fun," said Maisy, and climbed up after the wood elf.

Katy hesitated. The rope looked like it could break at any moment. Then, remembering what Jack had said, she began to climb.

Chapter 13. Treetop Prison

Lillian pressed her face against a crack in the fence but couldn't see through. She looked at the ruby gold flames flickering high above. The crackling sounded like the fire was laughing at her.

She turned around. The darkness of the forest beyond the clearing was even darker now. She felt like monsters were waiting for her to walk into the blackness. Instead, Lillian began to walk around the fence. She walked, walked, and walked, but didn't find a way in. She didn't even know where she had started walking. It all looked the same.

She bent down and drew an X in the dirt. As she started walking again, she thought about Katy, Maisy, and Jack. *What are the elves doing with them? I have to help, but I can't even get inside!*

The rope ladder swayed and bounced as Maisy and Katy climbed. The wooden rungs felt thin and rough in their hands.

"Isn't this awesome?" Maisy called down to Katy.

"No," said Katy in a nervous voice.

"I can see the whole elf village!"

"I don't like seeing the whole elf village," said Katy. She stopped climbing and looked down. The elves scurried, worked, and played. She didn't see Jack anywhere.

The elf below her yelled and hit her shoe with its clawed hand. Katy gasped and began to climb again. She felt like the ladder could break at any moment.

Katy looked up past Maisy and the lead elf. The rope ladder ended at the flat bottom of a tree house, with a little trapdoor on metal hinges. The trapdoor was closed.

The lead elf stopped. One of its hands stayed on the last rung as the other reached into a pocket and pulled out the same rock it had used to open the wall. It touched the rock to the trapdoor. Click! The elf pushed the trapdoor open and climbed inside the tree house.

Maisy climbed in, followed by Katy. The elf grabbed the trapdoor, swung down onto the ladder, and slammed the door shut, leaving them alone. Click!

"I don't like that sound at all," said Maisy.

"We're in jail!" said Katy. "What did we do wrong?!"

"We followed Lillian," Maisy scoffed, but secretly she was having the time of her life.

It was dim inside. The entire cell was painted black

and there were only four small windows, one in each wall.

"Look," said Katy. "Windows. Jack said elves don't like windows."

"That's why they use them in prisons," said Maisy.

Katy looked out a window and sighed. "My poor parents. They must be so worried."

"Hello," said a lilting voice from behind them.

Katy and Maisy spun around. A rusty metal cage hung from the ceiling. Inside sat a dryad. Her long hair was made of slender vines covered with green leaves and purple passion flowers.

"Make yourselves at home," she said with a sad smile. "You'll be here for a long time."

After an hour, Lillian returned to the X. She had walked around the entire fort. There was no way in.

Lillian sat in the dirt and stared up at the wall. She knew there was no way to climb over, and it would take too long to dig under.

She heard something behind her. Frightened, she jumped to her feet and turned, but all she saw was the gloomy forest. Nothing moved. Lillian listened, but didn't hear anything. After staring into the darkness for several long seconds, she turned back to the wall. Right away she heard the same noise again, like the wind blowing through a bush. She spun around. Again, all she saw was the black forest, but the sound grew louder.

Then suddenly the sound stopped and someone stepped out from behind a tree. It was the dryad they had met when they first entered the forest, the one with the white flowers.

"Anemone?" said Lillian.

The dryad motioned for Lillian to come closer. She ran through the clearing.

"Lillian," whispered Anemone. "Why didn't you go home?"

Lillian was surprised that Anemone remembered her name. "My friends were captured by the creatures who live here."

"Those are wood elves. They're never going to let your friends go. The elves are probably eating one of them right now."

Lillian gasped. "Eating—?!"

"I can help you get inside," said Anemone. "But you have to promise to save my friend, Passiflora. She's also a prisoner."

"Why can't you go inside?"

"The wood elves use their magic nets to capture dryads. They force us to control the trees. That's how they made this clearing and the fort."

Lillian turned and stared at the huge wall. *If I go in there and get caught by the wood elves, I'll get eaten too. But if I don't go, they'll eat Katy, Maisy, and Jack—all because I was too scared to help.*

"OK, you get me over that fence and I'll free your friend. If I can."

Anemone leaned closer. "You have to promise."

Lillian hesitated. "I promise."

"Come with me."

Anemone led Lillian to the far side of the fence.

"Stay here," she said.

The dryad ran back to the edge of the forest and stopped by a tree that was taller and wider than a giant Sequoia. She gently placed both hands on the trunk, smiled up at the tree, and gave it a small nudge.

The soil rippled like water as the tree silently glided away from the forest. Lillian stared and took a step back as the tree flowed through the clearing, towering above her. It stopped about five yards from the wall.

The dryad stepped from behind the tree. "Ready?"

Lillian looked from the tree to the dryad. "Ready for what?"

The dryad touched the tree again. To Lillian's amazement, a huge branch bent down. She stepped back again, but bumped into the wall. She watched as the branch, with a low creaking and rustling, came to her like a giant, leafy hand. It stopped by her knees.

"Sit on the branch," said Anemone. "The tree will lift you over the wall."

Lillian looked up. "What if I fall?"

"The tree will catch you," said Anemone.

That doesn't make me feel any safer, thought Lillian. She swung her leg over the branch like she was getting on a horse. She grabbed two long twigs for balance.

"Remember your promise," whispered Anemone.

Suddenly, the branch rose up into the air. The twigs snapped off in her hands as Lillian bolted in surprise.

She fell forward and hugged the branch like a koala bear. Anemone got smaller and smaller as the tree lifted Lillian higher and higher.

The branch carried Lillian above the wall. She saw scores of two-foot flames blazing atop the highest posts. She felt heat coming off the nearest flames.

As the branch lifted Lillian over the wall, she had a view of the whole village. She saw elves working and playing—and she saw Jack tied to a tree! He wasn't far from her end of the fort.

Then the branch lowered her down the other side. A huge fence, half as high as the wall, stood between her and the rest of the village. As Lillian sank behind the fence, she smelled something rotten.

She looked down. Dark, lumpy, moldy meat, along with bones, bits of rope, and broken tools, all lay piled beneath her. The closer she came to the ground, the stronger the stench grew.

The branch shook Lillian off like a bug. With a gasp she tumbled through the air and landed on her back, sinking into the squishy, reeking heap.

The putrid smell was so strong Lillian's eyes watered. She jumped to her feet and whacked soggy chunks of flesh off the backs of her arms and legs.

This must be where the elves put their trash, she thought. *I guess the dryad dropped me here so no one would see me.*

Lillian staggered through the thick stuff. With each step, she squelched into the pile of garbage up to her knees. She bit her lip so she wouldn't gag.

There were two small openings at either end of the fence. Lillian approached one side, peered around, and saw elves carrying tools, spears, and nets. Beyond the elves, she saw Jack tied with his back to a tree.

Lillian ducked behind the wall and knelt on the ground. She took off her backpack, unzipped the top, and grabbed her pocketknife. She zipped the pack and swung it on her back. Carefully, she pulled one blade out of the pocketknife.

Lillian felt scared. She tried to encourage herself. *I can save my friends. I can do it, I can do it, I can do it.*

She peeked around the corner and waited for the right moment. *As soon as the elves turn their backs—*

Before she could finish her thought, the right moment came. The elves were all walking away. She took a deep breath, then bolted.

Katy and Maisy sat in front of the dryad's cage.

"How did you get here?" asked Katy.

"A few years back," said the dryad, "I was sitting by a pond, eating fruit with other dryads and gossiping about the monsters in the forest. We were surprised by a big pack of wood elves. My friends escaped, but the elves caught me in a net and dragged me away."

"Why didn't you use magic and turn into a tree?" asked Katy.

"The elves would have waited until I turned back."

"Can't you stay a tree as long as you want?"

The dryad sighed. "If we stay a tree too long, we turn into a tree forever. We begin to feel the way a tree feels. We sink our roots deep into the earth and feel the sun warm our branches and the wind rustle our leaves. We slip into ancient time. Everything slows down. If a dryad stays that way too long, her soul goes to sleep forever and there's no way to wake her up."

"Being a tree doesn't sound so bad," said Maisy.

"It's not, but you don't have your own personality," said the dryad. "You're not *you* anymore."

"Oh," said Maisy. "But I'm my favorite person."

"The last dryad made this entire elf fort," said Passiflora. "They kept her a prisoner for a hundred years. But once they caught me, they let her go."

Katy's face softened with compassion. "How could a dryad make all this?"

"Dryads can control trees," said Passiflora, her eyes brightening. "We can make trees grow just by touching the soil. We can make trees move just by touching their bark. That's why I'm in this cage. The windows are sealed and the floor is clean. The elves don't want a branch to grow through the window or dirt to pile up on the floor. That's all I would need to escape. When the elves take me out to work, they tie my hands and hold knives to my throat and axes to my feet. There's no chance to get away."

"I wish we could help you," said Katy.

"We can!" said Maisy.

She pulled a bobby pin out of Katy's hair.

"Hey!" said Katy.

Maisy walked up to the cage, grabbed the lock and inserted the end of the clip. As Maisy fiddled with the lock, the dryad smiled at Katy and Katy smiled back.

Katy's foot itched. She took off her shoe and rubbed her toes. A small pile of dirt spilled out of her shoe onto the well-swept floor.

Remembering what the dryad had said, Katy jerked her head up and stared at the dryad with wide eyes. "Can you use *this* dirt?"

The dryad looked sad. "That's not enough."

Katy scooped up the dirt, stood, walked over to the dryad, and placed the pinch of dirt into the cage. She took off her other shoe, turned it over and tapped out the dirt.

"Maisy, take off your shoes," said Katy urgently.

Maisy still worked at the lock. "Can't you see I'm busy? This stupid lock!"

"Maisy!" shouted Katy. "Take off your shoes!"

Maisy stopped and looked at Katy. "Why?"

"Just give me your shoes!"

Maisy dropped the hair pin, took off her shoes and handed them to Katy.

Katy emptied the dirt from Maisy's shoes into the dryad's cage, making a little mound of dark soil.

"That," said the dryad with a hopeful smile, "should be enough." She touched the dirt with one long finger.

The girls watched in wonder as a tree began to grow.

Chapter 14. A Tree Behind Bars

Jack stood with his back pressed against the tree, his arms stretched around the trunk like he was hugging the tree backwards. Thin cords, twisted into a rope, had been wrapped from his wrists halfway up his forearms. He couldn't move at all.

Out of the corner of his eye, Jack saw a blur of red hair as Lillian darted across the open space. He was surprised and impressed. *How did she get over the wall? She's more capable than I thought.*

Lillian crouched behind the tree.

"Shhh," she whispered. "It's me."

"I know," Jack murmured under his breath. "Smells like you were in the trash."

"It was disgusting."

"Good. The stink will hide your human scent."

Lillian cut at the ropes with her knife, waiting for the strands to fray. But nothing happened.

"Don't worry," she said.

She folded the blade back into the pocketknife. Using her thumb and index finger, she pried out a serrated blade. She tapped the sharp teeth and quickly drew her finger back, watching as a drop of blood rose onto her skin.

I hope this works, she thought.

She sawed at the rope, but it was like using a butter knife. She tried again. *This should be working! Knives cut rope! That's how the world works!*

Lillian stopped. *But I'm not in my world anymore.*

"These aren't normal ropes," said Jack. "Elven ropes are woven with magic. You need an elf knife. The ropes even stop me from using my own powers."

"You can do magic?" asked Lillian.

"A little," said Jack.

Lillian leaned against the tree. *He probably could have escaped if it wasn't for Katy, Maisy, and me.*

She felt discouraged. Peeking around the tree, she saw elves coming toward them. She ducked back and listened. *Did they see me?*

Jack watched grimly as the elves carried big pieces of firewood to a ring of blackened stones. They put the wood in a circle like the spokes of a wheel. Each piece of wood was stripped of bark and neatly cut four feet long and one foot wide. On either side of the pit, sturdy Y-shaped sticks had been pounded into the ground. A metal bar lay across the sticks, grimy and crusted with dried meat.

Peering around the tree, Lillian watched as an elf walked up to the pit. It pulled a pouch out of its pocket. The little bag was made of green silk with a drawstring of blue ribbon. Lillian almost gasped aloud. *That belongs to Bluebell!*

The elf opened the bag and shook out two octagon-shaped diamonds, each about an inch tall and half an inch wide. The diamonds were polished clear; there wasn't even a scratch on them. One tip of each diamond had been chiseled off, leaving a flat edge.

"What's going on?" whispered Lillian from behind the tree. She had never seen such diamonds before.

Jack watched the elf touch the two flat ends of the diamonds together, then pull them apart. Blue and white flames burst from the space between the gems. The fire lit one log, then another, wrapping around the edges of the wood. With a whoosh, the flames spread.

"The elves are making a dinner fire," said Jack.

"What are they going to cook?" asked Lillian.

"Me," he said.

Katy and Maisy stared in awe as the little tree inside the dryad's cage grew. Branches reached up like they were stretching after a long night's sleep. Smaller twigs sprouted and tiny, green leaves unfolded. In just a few seconds, the tree was five feet tall. Orange and yellow leaves appeared in the sea of green. The branches thickened and curved to stay inside the cage. The dryad sat under the tree, smiling up at it.

The tree coiled a strong branch around one of the rusty metal bars, tightened like a fist, and pulled. The bar bent with a low creak—Snap! Bits of metal shot into the room as the bar broke in half. The two pieces fell on the floor at Maisy's feet.

"Well, well, well, what do we have here?" grinned Maisy. She picked up the smaller bar and slapped it against the palm of her hand. "Those stupid elves will run when they see the all-powerful Maisy with her new weapon!"

Katy rolled her eyes.

The dryad stepped out of the cage and stretched. "I'm free!" She turned to Katy. "Thank you for saving me."

Katy smiled at the dryad, then walked over to the window. "We could probably use the bars to break the glass, then we can all get out of here."

Katy looked out the window. They were about one hundred feet high and she could see most of the village. She watched the little elves far below but she was too high to see what they were doing. Katy lifted her head. She saw other trees nearby with more tree houses. Elves climbed up and down and gathered on the porches. They looked like they were talking and arguing.

"These elves are always angry, aren't they?"

Katy followed the lines of the trees down to the ground—and saw Jack tied to a trunk.

"Look! It's Jack!"

"Let me see!" said Maisy. She pushed Katy away from the window and stared out. "There's a big fire."

Passiflora looked out another window. "They're going to eat him for dinner."

"What?!" shouted Katy. "Can you help him?"

"I can try," said Passiflora. She touched the wall of the prison.

Katy and Maisy felt a tremble go through the tree.

"The other trees are moving!" shouted Maisy.

Katy pressed her face next to Maisy's. Through the window, they saw a branch slowly bend toward the right and touch the tree next to it. That tree reached out a thin branch and touched the next tree. The branches stretched from tree to tree; some leaves fell as the branches moved quicker and quicker. It looked like a green wave rippling across the sky. The branches hit the tree Jack was tied to. The tree trembled like it was waking up. Its branches quivered and a small shiver moved down its trunk.

Lillian crouched behind the tree. She heard fire crackling. *What am I going to do?*

Jack stared at the blue and green flames. The elves used mortars and pestles to grind leaves and berries into spices. Every once in a while, one of the elves glanced up at Jack hungrily.

Lillian pressed her hands against the rough bark and peeked around the trunk. "I don't know how to help you," she whispered.

Before Jack could answer, he felt the tree tremble at his back. Lillian felt it too, like a cat purring against her palms. She jumped back and clasped her hands over her mouth to stop herself from crying out.

She stared in amazement as four bumps swelled on the trunk right in front of her, two above and two below the ropes. The bumps moved like fists trying to punch through the bark, then four bare branches grew. They shot straight out of the tree, each about five feet long, barely missing Lillian as she jumped away. The branches curved back toward the ropes. Lillian ducked, scrabbling backwards.

The branches coiled around the ropes. Two pulled one way and two pulled the other. At first it looked like the branches were playing tug-of-war. Lillian heard a low creaking as the ropes quivered.

Snap! The ropes flew apart. The elves looked up, surprised. They charged toward Jack, thrusting their spears and shaking their nets.

"Wait here," Jack ordered Lillian.

Then he ran at the elves who were running at him. The elves stopped, confused. Some of the smaller elves turned and ran, while the bigger elves bunched together like a wall of bones, clutching their spears. They waited for Jack.

But right before he impaled himself on their spears, Jack leapt.

Watching from behind the tree, Lillian saw his arms grow longer, his fingers turn into feathers, his nose stretch into a beak—and suddenly Jack was a human-sized hawk, bronze and angry. With an earsplitting screech, he rose into the air.

The elves stumbled back, jabbing their spears franticly. The sweep of the hawk's wings knocked them to the ground. They watched as their dinner rose higher and higher.

Lillian stared, transfixed. "A *little* magic?" she whispered to herself, remembering what Jack had said.

Up in the tree, Maisy and Katy stared as Jack flew straight up, his powerful wings beating the air. He flashed past their window.

Maisy pressed her cheek against the glass, looking up, trying to see where Jack went. "That was awesome!"

Katy turned toward Passiflora. "I didn't know Jack had powers!"

The dryad smiled at the girls. "I imagine there's a lot you don't know about Jack."

Chapter 15. Escape

From high above, Jack saw the entire village. He dove back down toward the elves. He felt like a comet, plummeting to earth.

The elves ducked as Jack pulled up inches from their bony heads. They watched as the hawk flapped his powerful wings, ascending into the air. The elves grabbed their nets, spears, bows, and arrows.

Lillian's eyes followed Jack. As he banked behind the prison tree house, she saw three faces in the small windows. Two of the faces she recognized.

"Katy and Maisy!" she whispered to herself.

The third face was a dryad like Anemone.

As Jack flew toward the wall surrounding the fort, an arrow shot past his wing. He tilted to the side and looked over his feathery shoulder. Elves frantically fit arrows to bows. A spear punched into a tree below him. Swerving and pitching, Jack dodged spears and arrows. The sharp missiles whizzed by like a deadly wind, thunking into trees or arcing back to the ground. A few embedded into tree houses; elves ran out of their leafy dens, yelling curses, rushing down rope ladders to join the hunt.

Jack soared over the wall. One elf pulled the rough rock out of its pocket and pressed it to the wall. Two logs sprung up into the air. The elves raced out. Thud! The logs dropped back, locking down the village.

A blue sky stretched above the clearing. The elves threw spears and shot arrows, but Jack soared away between the trees. The elves swarmed into the darkness of the forest, shouting and cursing.

Lillian looked up at the prison and saw Maisy and Katy in one of the windows. She rushed over to the tree. The ladder leading up had thin, frayed ropes and weather-worn rungs.

As Lillian grabbed onto a rung, the tree shook. She jumped back in surprise and looked up. A small, round hole appeared in the tree between the two windows. The opening grew until it was as big and round as a hobbit door.

Through the opening, Lillian saw Katy and Maisy. Katy smiled and waved, and Maisy raised the metal bar and shook it like a crazed wood elf. Lillian laughed.

The dryad appeared between Katy and Maisy,

touched the opening, and stepped over the edge into empty space, as if she intended to walk across the air. A short branch suddenly grew out of the tree, sprouting a giant leaf that unfurled in the shape of a golden star. The leaf bent as the dryad carelessly stepped onto its smooth surface, sat down on the end, and slid off like a dew drop. Another branch grew out of the tree; another golden leaf opened right under her and she slid onto it. A silver vein grew down the middle of the first leaf and the sides curled up like a slide.

Branch after branch grew below her, each a little longer than the one before, and each producing a golden leaf. As the dryad slid down faster and faster, silver veins grew down the center of the curling leaves.

That looks like fun! thought Lillian.

The dryad slid off the last leaf and landed on her feet next to Lillian.

Lillian laughed. "Wow."

The dryad smiled, then turned and beckoned for Katy and Maisy to follow. Katy stepped back, but without a thought Maisy jumped onto the giant leaf.

"Maisy!" yelled Katy.

Maisy slipped, landed on her rear, and sped down the leaves, gently bumping from leaf to leaf. *This is better than the giant slide at the County Fair!*

"Yeah!" Maisy whooped, shaking the metal bar over her head. "Whoo hoo!"

Maisy zipped down the leaves and slid onto the dirt. As she stood up, Lillian hugged her.

"I'm so glad you're alive!" said Lillian.

Maisy gently pushed Lillian off. "I'm glad to see you too, but you know I don't hug."

High above, Katy stood at the edge of the opening. She wondered how easy it would be to break through one of the leaves or go flying off while sliding down. It looked unsafe and as fast as a ride at Six Flags. She never liked fast rides.

"What are you waiting for?!" Maisy shouted.

Some of the smaller elves came to watch. They didn't look dangerous, but more kept arriving.

Katy carefully sat on the edge with her feet touching the first leaf. She eased herself onto the smooth, golden surface, and slowly pushed herself forward. She could see everything from here. Maisy, Lillian, and the dryad looked as small as action figures.

Katy reached the end of the leaf. She had one second of terror as the leaf dipped … then she zipped down the slide with a scream. The wind blew her hair behind her and her stomach dropped into her feet.

Maisy laughed. "This is what I live for."

Katy flew down the leafy slide, screaming all the way. She tumbled off the last leaf into the dirt, rolled, and bumped to a stop against Maisy's legs.

Lillian extended a hand. Katy just lay on the ground for a minute, dazed.

"Are you OK?" asked Lillian.

Katy took Lillian's hand and stood up. "No."

Maisy burst out laughing. "For years I've been

trying to get you on a roller coaster! If I knew that all I had to do was force you into a magical world and get you captured by wood elves, we would have come here a lot sooner!"

Lillian smiled and hugged Katy.

"We need to go," said the dryad. "The warrior elves will return soon."

By now, thirty or forty small elves were watching, but they didn't want to mess with Passiflora.

As they grabbed their backpacks, Lillian picked up an elf knife. The dryad led them to a tree near the wall. She placed her hands on the trunk. The tree tilted toward them like it was falling. Leaves rained down as the tree noisily pulled its branches away from its neighbors.

Katy, Maisy, and Lillian expected it to break any second. They turned to run, but the small elves were behind them, watching.

The girls turned back. The tree creaked, bending over like a person who had dropped something, and wrapped one big branch around the dryad and the girls like it was giving them a hug.

Lillian watched with a surprised smile as the branch bent around their waists as smoothly as her own arm.

"Wow …"

Katy pushed on the branch, but it just pulled her closer to the trunk.

"Wait wait wait!" said Katy.

"Go go go!" said Maisy.

"Hold on," said Passiflora.

The tree slowly stood, lifting them into the air. Katy wrapped one arm around the thick branch and grabbed some twigs with her other hand. Lillian held two small branches, while Maisy leaned over the bough, shaking her metal bar at the wood elves below.

"Good riddance! You're not worth another word, else I'd call you knave!"

Lillian grinned at Katy.

The tree carefully lifted them toward the blue sky, then the branch reached over the wall and stretched down the other side.

Once the girls could feel the ground under their feet again, the branch opened and let them go. They watched as the branch moved halfway back up the wall, then stopped. It was just a branch again, no longer under the dryad's spell.

They all ran into the forest.

"Passiflora?" said a voice from the darkness. Another dryad stepped out from behind a tree.

"Anemone!" said Passiflora.

"It's nice to see you too," said Anemone. "I knew you could escape with a little help!"

"Yes, I couldn't have done it without these girls," said Passiflora, smiling at Maisy and Katy.

"Maybe I was wrong about you and your sister," Anemone said to Lillian. "I'll tell the dryad council about this."

"I have much to tell them too," said Passiflora. "I know what the elves are up to."

"Where will you go now?" asked Lillian.

"Deep into the forest," said Passiflora, then pointed straight ahead. "But you, keep walking that way and you'll find your way home."

"Let's go," said Maisy.

"Thank you for helping us," said Katy.

"No," said Passiflora, "thank *you*. Without you, I'd still be in that prison."

"We are both grateful," Anemone added. "But your ill-mannered friend is right, you should go before the elves come back."

"*I'm* ill-mannered?" said Maisy. "Are you serious? A metal monster tried to kill us, Medusa tried to shoot us, the Kraken tried to destroy us, the salamander thingy tried to eat me, the chimera wanted to eat me and so did the elves, and your friend here lied to us! And *I'm* ill-mannered?!"

"Calm down," said Lillian. "You have a point but so does the dryad. You *can* be rude sometimes."

"Sometimes?" muttered Katy under her breath.

They waved and said goodbye to the dryads, then the girls walked away.

Jack glided farther into the gloomy forest, swerving around trees. He didn't fly his fastest because he wanted the elves to follow, so the girls would have a chance to escape. He banked on his outstretched wings and saw the dry river bed below.

The angry elves followed him across. The rocks

hurt their feet, slowing them down. They ran faster again on the other side, shouting and cursing in their nasally voices.

Jack felt an arrow pass harmlessly through his wing feathers. He pulled straight up, weaving between branches and disappearing into the roof of leaves. Everything went dark as he fought his way through. He saw cracks of light far above. Pounding the leafy air, he bolted upward and burst through into the warmth of the bright sun. He leveled off and surveyed a green sea, spread for miles below him. Everything looked beautiful.

Jack dipped his wings and flew back toward the fort. Far ahead, he saw the small hole of the clearing. *I hope I'm not too late.*

He dove down into the clearing, glided over the wall and into the village. He flew to the tree near the fire, but Lillian wasn't there. Flapping his bronze wings, he landed on the ground. Jack the hawk looked up at the prison and the slide of golden leaves. The dirt under the last leaf was scuffed with footprints. *It looks like a dryad helped the girls escape.*

Four sets of prints led away. He followed, his bird body moving from side to side as he walked. The footprints ended at the wall. He looked up and saw a tree with one big branch stretched over the wall as if it was grabbing for something on the other side. Jack felt relieved.

He heard yelling behind him. Looking over his shoulder, he saw the warrior elves had returned from the forest and were running toward him. Jack flapped his wings. Dirt, ash, and bits of debris clouded up, making a small storm, wiping away the girls' footprints.

Jack flew over the wall, leaving the exhausted elves behind.

Chapter 16. Two Rescues

Lillian, Katy, and Maisy ran through the dim forest, determined to get as far away from the elves as they could. They hurried between shadowy trunks that emerged out of the darkness. The trees seemed to glide forward as silhouettes, becoming more detailed until the girls could see moss growing on the bark before the trees disappeared again behind them.

No glowing fruit in this part of the forest, thought Lillian. *We're going to get hungry soon.*

Tired and out of breath, Katy and Maisy stopped and sat on the ground.

"We have to keep going," said Lillian.

"We're exhausted," said Katy.

"I know, but the elves are still after us."

"We're far enough," said Maisy between breaths.

"We at least have to walk," said Lillian.

Katy got up. "She's right. If the elves see our footprints, they can find us."

"Come on, Maisy," said Lillian.

"I'm staying here," said Maisy, crossing her arms.

"Fine," said Katy. "Stay."

Lillian and Katy turned and walked away.

"I have great friends," called Maisy. "Leaving me in the middle of the forest. All alone. To be eaten."

Lillian and Katy kept walking.

Maisy tried again. "You *need* me!" She held up the metal bar. "I have the only weapon. You're safer with me!"

Lillian and Katy kept walking. They were just shadows in the gloom of the forest. Another few steps and they'd be gone.

"Fine, I'll come!" Maisy shouted. "But only because I need to protect you!" She ran to catch up, muttering curses as they walked deeper into the dark forest.

"Look!" said Lillian. She pointed at human footprints trampled by scores of smaller elf prints.

"This is where they blindfolded us," said Maisy.

They followed the footprints for a while until they heard a scraping noise. They stopped and listened. Now they could hear an animal whimpering. Katy moved toward the sound.

"Wait," said Lillian. "We don't know what it is."

Katy held a finger to her lips. "Shhh." *I think I know what's making that sound,* she thought.

She moved slowly forward and peeked around a

tree. Lillian and Maisy crept up behind her and looked over her shoulder. All three girls stared, then Lillian took a step back.

It was the chimera, bigger than an elephant and splayed across the dirt, still bound by the net.

"Katy, come on, let's go!" said Maisy.

Instead, Katy took a step toward the chimera. "We can't just leave him here to starve."

"Yes, we can," said Maisy. She reached for the back of Katy's jacket, but missed. "Let's get out of here."

Lillian grabbed Katy's arm. "Even if you can help the chimera, it'll probably eat you."

Katy gently removed Lillian's hand. She walked up from behind the chimera. The snake turned its triangular head to look at Katy through the small holes in the net. It hissed as she cautiously walked past. The goat watched closely, then made a miserable little, "Baa …"

Such a strange creature, thought Katy. *The lion and the snake are so scary, and the goat is so gentle.*

The lion growled, its fearsome red eyes staring at her through the net.

"It's OK, I'm not going to hurt you," soothed Katy as she slowly approached.

"Katy and animals," Maisy said, shaking her head. "Even here, she has to stop for stray cats."

The chimera's growl rumbled louder as Katy moved closer. She was only inches from the huge, shaggy head. She slowly reached out one hand. The chimera's muscles bulged as it tried to get away from Katy's touch. The ropes creaked and the wood stakes in the ground trembled.

"Let's get out of here!" said Lillian.

"It's about to break free!" shouted Maisy.

Katy turned and held a finger to her lips, then turned back to the chimera.

"It's OK," she said as she reached out her hand. "I'm going to help you." She stroked behind its ear with the tips of her fingers. The fur was tangled and rough. The chimera watched Katy.

She took off her backpack, opened it, and pulled out a bag of dried fruit. She dumped the fruit through the holes in the net. The chimera sniffed at it, then licked up chunks of mangoes, bananas, and blueberries.

Katy smiled. "You must be starving."

Maisy whispered to Lillian, "Why did Katy give our fruit to the bloodthirsty monster?"

"It's not a monster," said Katy, walking back to her friends. "It's a chimera." She reached into Lillian's backpack and slipped out the pocketknife. But Lillian handed her the small elf blade instead.

"Elven ropes are magic," she said.

"Thanks," said Katy. She held the rough blade in front of her. The chimera growled.

"It's OK," said Katy.

She grabbed one of the ropes. The chimera struggled, trying to get away from the knife. Katie petted it again. "I'm not going to hurt you," she said, and started sawing. The chimera snarled.

"It's working," Katy murmured in relief. Strand by strand, she cut the net. The chimera stopped growling as the net loosened. Katy cut one last rope, dropped the blade, and slowly backed up.

The chimera shook the net off its shoulders. Using its front paws, it dragged the rest of its body out of the net. It stood, stretched, and turned toward Katy.

"Run!" shouted Maisy.

Katy stood paralyzed with fear, but deep down she felt happy. It was the kind of happiness that makes you warm inside, the kind that seems to tell you, *You just did something great.*

The chimera bent down toward her. Katy's eyes widened as the lion's face came closer. Its mane smelled like the earth. She felt its warm breath stir her hair. It rubbed its big, powerful head against her like a cat, almost knocking her to the ground.

Katy laughed. She reached out one hand and petted the chimera behind its ear. "What's you're name?"

The chimera closed its eyes and purred. It sounded like a cat, only louder. Katy's hand vibrated as she ran her fingers through its fur.

"Do chimera's have names?" Katy asked as she petted its forehead.

"Don't name it!" groaned Maisy.

Lillian watched with a smile.

"I'm going to name you ... Fred," said Katy.

"Fred?!" shouted Maisy. "Fred is the name of a stuffed animal!"

"We have to go now," said Lillian.

"Bye, Fred," sighed Katy. She gave him one last scratch, then walked back toward the girls. But the chimera followed.

Katy turned back. "I'm leaving now." She started walking again. But still, he followed her. "Do you want to come with us?" Katy asked.

"Are you crazy?!" yelled Maisy. "That thing can't come with us."

"Yes, he can," said Katy. "And his name is Fred."

Maisy turned to Lillian. "Are you going to just stand there? Aren't you going to do something? This isn't like those stray animals she's always bringing home!"

"It might be handy," said Lillian, "to have a chimera on our side."

Maisy stared at Lillian in disbelief. "Our side?! He's on the hungry side! We're on the meat side!"

Lillian walked toward Katy and the chimera. She slowly reached out and touched him.

"Fred," said Katy, "this is Lillian. Lillian, this is Fred."

"Hi, Fred," said Lillian. She ran her fingers through his mane. The chimera purred.

Maisy walked out to join them. "After the chimera eats us and we're in heaven, I'll remind you guys that this was all your fault."

But Lillian felt safer with the chimera around. *He'll protect us,* she thought. *We're in this forest alone. We don't have Jack anymore. We don't know what's in here and we don't know how to get out.*

The chimera perked his ears and stared into the blackness between the trees. The girls followed his gaze.

A pack of wood elves emerged out of the shadows. Their white, translucent skin made them look like ghosts, or a dream. But their spears looked very dangerous and very real.

Jack flew through the dim forest, gliding around trees. He looked and listened for anything that might give him a hint of where the girls might be.

And then he saw something—three sets of human footprints. As he turned to follow, he heard a distant roar that could only come from the chimera. Then he heard a scream. It sounded like Katy.

There were ten elves in this small hunting party. They walked toward the girls, then stopped about five yards away when they saw the chimera. No one moved. One of the elves said something to the others. Several elves pointed spears at the girls and the others nodded.

The elves strode forward, spears straight ahead, arrows sliding from quivers. Before the girls could do anything, the chimera stepped in front of them like a guard dog. He growled.

One of the elves shook its spear at the chimera and yelled something. The rest of the elves echoed the battle cry and charged. Lillian grabbed Katy and Maisy and pulled them behind a tree.

The elves jabbed at the chimera with their spears.

The chimera swiped a huge paw, knocking the spears out of their bony fists. Other elves shot arrows but the pointed shafts glanced off the chimera's thick, tawny fur. The chimera roared.

The elves spread out, surrounding the chimera. An elf picked up a spear and jabbed at the snake. The snake hissed and dodged and struck. Snap! The snake caught the elf in its big jaws and threw the skeletal creature high in the air. The elf somersaulted, yelling in a terrified voice, before the lion caught and swallowed it, bones and all.

The girls watched from behind the tree. Katy was worried about Fred. Lillian was scared, but also curious. *This is like a Harryhausen movie,* she thought.

Maisy stepped out from behind the tree to get a better view. "This is awesome!" she murmured.

Elves scurried up nearby trees. One jumped, holding a spear over its head. But the chimera struck the elf in the air. The elf flew over Maisy's head and slammed against the tree that Lillian and Katy hid behind. The girls gasped as the elf fell to the ground, unconscious.

Maisy knelt on the ground and poked it curiously. "Ew, it feels like a bony lizard."

"Don't touch it!" whispered Katy.

Maisy noticed the knife in its belt. She grabbed the handle and pulled it out. The stone blade was only six inches long. Maisy held it like a little dagger.

"Maisy, behind you!" warned Lillian.

An elf had dodged around the chimera and was walking toward them. Maisy stood, hid the metal bar behind her back, and raised the knife. The short elf marched up and pointed its spear at her stomach. They stared at each other, then Maisy dropped the knife like she was giving up. The elf smiled. But suddenly, Maisy grabbed the spear's shaft with her free hand, swung the metal bar from behind her back, and bashed the elf on the side of its head. The elf's eyes rolled up and it fell to the ground.

"That's what you get for messing with the all-powerful Maisy," she grinned as she picked up its spear.

Lillian and Katy laughed. Then Katy saw something flash—from behind a tree soared a giant hawk.

"Look!" said Katy, pointing. "It's Jack!"

They watched the huge bird swoop down to join the battle.

"He found us!" said Lillian.

Jack snatched one elf in each claw, flew straight up toward the treetops, and let go. The elves howled until they hit the ground with a thud.

The five remaining elves looked around and saw a giant hawk swooping down, a roaring chimera ready to pounce, and Maisy running forward waving a metal bar. The elves exchanged glances, then turned and ran.

The fight was over.

Chapter 17. A Sister's Memory

The girls watched as Jack's wings grew shorter. Five feathers on either wing shrank and curled into fingers. The beak shortened into a human nose and the wide, alert eyes narrowed and lengthened. In seconds, Jack was himself again.

"Jack!" Katy ran over and gave him a hug.

"I'm glad you're OK," he said, his eyes fixed on the chimera. He tried to move Katy behind him, but she pushed his arm away and walked over to the chimera.

"He's on our side now, Jack. His name is Fred."

Jack and the chimera stared at each other. "They don't pick sides," said Jack. "They just hunt."

"I told you," said Maisy.

Katy reached up and scratched his mane. "I freed him from the elf net. He won't hurt me."

Jack thought about what she said. He knew chimeras were smart. If Katy saved his life, maybe the chimera *would* protect her.

"I was against this from the start," said Maisy.

"Maisy," said Katy.

Lillian placed her hand on Jack's arm. "Fred just saved our lives."

Jack walked up to the chimera. "Nice to meet you, Fred. I'm Jack."

"He can't understand you," scoffed Maisy. "He's a stupid animal."

Fred turned his big head toward Maisy and growled.

"Be careful," said Jack. "Chimeras can understand any language." Then Jack turned to Lillian. "So, are you ready to continue the journey?"

Lillian looked at her two best friends. Katy smiled and leaned into the chimera, happy for the first time since they arrived. Maisy raised her eyebrows, shook the metal bar, and grinned like a wood elf. They both gave Lillian a little nod.

"Ready," said Lillian.

As they walked on through the forest, the trees stood in the dark like bars in a jail, trapping them in this strange world.

What is Bluebell up to? wondered Lillian yet again. *The more of this world I see, the more I think Bluebell would feel right at home. The elves almost remind me of her. She's daring and reckless and not afraid of anything.*

Lillian remembered a beautiful spring day. She was in her room, lying on the bed, looking at the white mulberry blossoms on the tree outside the window. In one hand she held a pencil and in the other a ten dollar bill. She had saved one hundred dollars to buy a new dress. She thought about what kind of dress she wanted as she doodled dresses on the bill. Her favorite doodle showed a plain dress with short sleeves and a belt. *Knock, knock, knock.* "Lillian," called Bluebell from outside the door. "It's time to go buy your dress!" Lillian jumped out of bed, unzipped her wallet, stuffed the money inside, and zipped it up again. She rushed downstairs where Bluebell was waiting. The mall was packed with people. In the first store, Lillian tried on a light green dress with two-inch straps and a dark green band around the waist. She liked this dress but she didn't buy it. In the next store, she tried on a light blue dress with long sleeves and a dark blue band; the bottom of the dress almost touched the floor. Then she saw the one she wanted: a flowing red dress with spaghetti straps. The top was plain, but it had a band of silver sequins and a pleated bottom that fell to her ankles. "That's a wonderful dress," said Bluebell. Lillian hung her purse on a hook and took the dress into the fitting room. She looked at herself in the mirror. Her red hair matched the red dress perfectly. She loved it. She rushed out of the dressing room to show her sister. "You look beautiful," said Bluebell. At the checkout counter, Lillian reached into her purse for her wallet. It wasn't there. She double checked. "My wallet's gone!" Bluebell turned and looked right at Lillian. "Someone must have stolen it," she said. The second Bluebell looked into her eyes, Lillian knew that her sister had taken it. They went to security, but there wasn't anything to do. Lillian was certain that Bluebell *knew* she knew. It was as if Bluebell was testing her, waiting to see if Lillian would tell or not.

Lillian thought about this memory as she followed Jack through the gloomy forest. *What was she trying to prove? She always did things for a reason. So why is she here? What does she want from this dark world?*

Lillian was afraid of the answer.

Jack, the chimera, and the girls walked for hours. The forest seemed to go on forever.

"Can we stop to rest?" asked Maisy.

"Not yet," said Jack. "We have to keep moving."

"Why? The elves are gone."

"Wood elves aren't the worst thing in this forest."

"Yeah? What's worse than those bony little devils?"

Jack shook his head. "You don't want to know."

"Shouldn't have said that," Lillian muttered under her breath.

Katy grinned.

Maisy walked faster to catch up with Jack. "I *do* want to know. Tell me."

"No."

"Come on."

"No."

"Please?"

"No."

Maisy tapped the metal bar on her palm. "If you don't tell me ..."

"You're not going to hit me."

"Fine. But for safety reasons, you should tell me."

"No."

"I should be informed about what lives here."

Jack ignored her now.

"I'll just keep talking until you tell me ... I can talk for a *long* time."

Jack didn't answer.

"I don't believe you, Jack. There's nothing worse than wood elves and this creature," she pointed behind her at the chimera. "You're just trying to scare me. But I don't scare, Jack. Let me give you an example. I watched *Jaws* without closing my eyes and then I went swimming at the beach, Jack. Are you listening, Jack?"

"Just tell her," sighed Katy.

Everyone stopped walking.

Jack turned to Maisy. "Flesh eating wendigos, parties of crazy satyrs, packs of ravenous wargs, and ghoulish aswangs who enjoy eating human hearts."

Maisy just looked at Jack for a long moment.

"I didn't need to know *that,*" she said.

Everyone rolled their eyes and started walking.

They were all tired and hungry and wanted to take a

break. It was always dark in the forest, so they felt like they had been walking all night.

Katy slowed down as she walked. The chimera noticed she was exhausted and nudged her shoulder. Katy turned. He bent down and put his head on the ground. Katy petted the top of his head. "Do you want some attention, Fred?"

She turned and started walking again. But the chimera grabbed Katy's backpack in his mouth and lifted her a few feet in the air.

"Hey!" Katy laughed. Everyone stopped and turned to watch.

Fred put Katy down. Confused, she looked into the chimera's brown eyes. "What do you want?"

Fred put his head under her elbow and pushed up.

"Do you want to give me a ride?" asked Katy.

Fred nodded. He bent his head to the ground again. Katy put one foot on his leg, placed her right hand on his shoulder, and grabbed his mane with her left hand. She pulled herself up and swung one leg over his back like she was mounting an elephant-sized horse. She grabbed onto his mane with both hands as Fred stood up.

"Wow!" said Katy.

"Amazing," said Lillian.

Jack shook his head. "Never thought I'd see a human riding a chimera."

"No fair!" said Maisy. "I wanna ride the chimera!"

Fred seemed to smile as he looked at Maisy.

Katy leaned toward Fred's ear. "Can my friends ride too?"

The chimera bent down again. Lillian climbed on behind Katy, reached a hand down to Maisy and helped her up. Fred stood, lifting the girls twelve feet in the air.

Lillian laughed. "I'm in a Ray Harryhausen movie!"

Maisy held up her bar. "I'm king of the world!"

Jack laughed. Suddenly, no one felt tired anymore. The dark forest seemed bright and magical again.

"Aren't you going to get on?" Katy asked Jack.

"No," said Jack. "I can keep up."

With a jump, Fred started to run, slowly at first, steadily gaining speed, faster and faster, lunging around the shadowy trunks. The girls bounced up and down and jerked back and forth. Katy clutched onto Fred's mane, Lillian hugged Katy tight around her waist, and Maisy held onto Lillian for dear life, laughing at the same time.

It was amazing to watch a tree rush straight at them out of the darkness, then suddenly jump out of the way as Fred bolted around it.

"This is better than Space Mountain!" crowed Maisy.

As they zipped through the forest, Lillian looked to the side. Jack ran right next to them, easily keeping pace as if he was jogging through a park. Lillian laughed.

The ride was bumpy, and after an hour the girls' legs were sore. Katy's fingers ached from holding on to the chimera's mane so tightly.

Far ahead, they saw what looked like a star in a black sky. As they galloped closer, the star grew into a moon.

Finally, they had reached the end of the forest.

They burst into bright sunlight. Jack and the chimera slowed down, then stopped running. The girls covered their eyes. After being in the dark forest so long, they couldn't see anything but white. As their eyes adjusted, they saw shapes, then colors.

Slowly the world came into view. All around them were beautiful foothills covered with green grass and colorful flowers—red and white roses, orange flame azaleas, Indian strawberry blossoms so tiny a dew drop would drown them, tulips so big you could sit inside them, surreal dahlias, and pink calla lilies as tall as Fred.

The chimera bent down and the girls slid off his back. They took a few steps forward, staring at this amazing sight.

Maisy looked up. "Whoa …"

"I know," said Katy. "The flowers are unbelievable!"

Maisy pointed upward. "No. Look."

Mountains, much bigger than Mount Everest, stood in the distance, a zigzag line of rocky crags stretching to the horizon. The base was brown, gray, and smooth. The middle range was rugged and lightly dusted with snow. The peaks were smooth and completely white; it looked like nature had tried to bury the mountains in snow.

A sunlit, cloudless blue sky spread over the foothills. But farther beyond, the sky over the mountains was black, lit by a full moon and stars. It looked like the mountains were in an invisible box filled with night and the foothills were in an invisible box flooded with day, and the boxes were pushed up against each other. The girls gazed at this mysterious sight.

Lillian turned to Jack. "This place keeps getting stranger and stranger."

Jack grinned. "The strangest is still to come."

Chapter 18. Edible Flowers

They walked a few yards away from the forest and sat down in a small patch of clover. Maisy unzipped her backpack and looked for something to eat, but her backpack was empty. She looked through every pocket but didn't find one crumb!

"Where's my food?!" she yelled.

Lillian unzipped her backpack. "I have your food, remember? I took it before we entered the forest." She pulled out a granola bar and handed it to Maisy.

Maisy gave Lillian the stink eye, but took the bar.

Katy offered a granola bar to Jack.

"I'm not really hungry," said Jack.

The girls ate granola bars and dried fruit. Lillian slid her water bottle out of a side pocket. She unscrewed the lid and took a sip. She was so thirsty that the water tasted better than anything she had ever tasted before. She took another sip, but only a few drops landed on her tongue. She looked at the shiny metal inside. The bottle was empty.

"Jack," asked Lillian, "is there a river nearby where we can refill our bottles?"

"There are springs," said Jack, "up in the foothills."

Maisy finished the last bite of her granola bar and put the wrapper in the side pocket of her backpack. "Let's go," she said. She wanted to explore the foothills, and especially the flowers.

Katy and Lillian were finished too. They collected their wrappers and zipped up their backpacks. Everybody stood up, ready to go.

Katy turned around. "Come on, Fred."

The chimera didn't move.

Katy walked back to Fred. She petted the chimera and looked into his eyes. "What's wrong?"

"Katy," said Jack. "Fred isn't coming with us."

"Why not?"

"Chimeras only leave the forest if they have to."

Katy put her arms around the chimera's mane. She didn't want Fred to leave. "Bye, Fred. See you on our way back."

"*If* we make it back," said Maisy.

Katy stroked the chimera's ears. Fred growled sadly, like a lonely purr. He nudged his head against Katy's chest, turned around and, without looking back, walked into the forest.

Katy watched until he disappeared into the darkness, then she followed Lillian, Maisy, and Jack toward the foothills.

All around stood huge tulips, calla lilies, and dahlias. The warm air smelled sweet from little red and white roses that grew over the grass.

The tulips bloomed low to the ground because the stems weren't strong enough to hold the flowers up. Lillian reached one hand out to touch a purple tulip the size of a bean bag chair.

"Don't touch the flowers," warned Jack.

"Why not?" said Maisy. "It's big, but it's just a flower."

Before anyone could say anything, Maisy stepped onto a big tulip petal. The thick petal bent under her weight. She felt like she was walking on a giant balloon.

"Get off the flower!" Jack ordered.

But Maisy just kept walking. Suddenly, the flower snapped shut on her like a Venus fly trap.

Maisy shouted, her voice echoing inside the giant tulip. "Hey! This stupid flower is eating me!"

Katy and Lillian laughed, but Jack rushed forward, grabbed one of the petals, and pulled. The top of the petal bent as the whole flower tilted toward him. He wrenched the petal as hard as he could. It slowly peeled open and Maisy rolled out with a thud.

She lay on the ground, dazed.

"Why don't you ever listen?" said Jack.

"Flowers aren't supposed to eat people!" said Maisy.

"Maybe not in your world," said Jack.

Katy and Lillian laughed so hard they were on the verge of tears.

Maisy looked up. "That wasn't funny."

"You're right," said Jack. "Look at your backpack."

The girls stopped laughing.

Maisy stood up and took off her backpack. Part of the strap had been dissolved inside the flower.

"What happened?" asked Maisy.

Katy pointed. "Look at the hem of your sleeve!"

Maisy lifted her arm. The sleeve was also partly dissolved, the edge frayed as if it had been chewed off.

"The plant *was* trying to eat you!" said Lillian. "I'm sorry we laughed."

"Why does everything in this world have to be dangerous?" asked Maisy.

Jack tapped Maisy on her shoulder. "From now on, are you going to do what I tell you?"

"Maybe," said Maisy.

"I'm serious," said Jack.

"Fine," said Maisy, secretly crossing her fingers behind her back.

Jack and the girls walked higher into the foothills, leaving the big flowers behind. Now the ground was covered in blankets of small roses, Indian strawberry blossoms, and flame azaleas.

"Why are there so many flowers here?" asked Katy.

"There might be a spring on this hill," said Jack.

"A spring?" said Lillian. "Jack, I'd like to fill our water bottles before we get into the mountains."

Jack nodded.

Then Lillian heard something. She stopped walking. "Shhh! Listen."

Everybody stopped. At first they heard nothing. The foothills felt as still as a painting. Then they heard running water.

They walked toward the sound. Maisy felt cold water seep into her right shoe. "What the heck," she said. She stepped out of the small stream. "I found the water."

Lillian knelt by the brook. She took off her backpack, pulled out her water bottle and unscrewed the lid. She was disappointed that the spring was so small. It was only six inches wide, with a plain, muddy bottom. She held the bottle under and watched water flow into it, then took a sip. The water was ice cold and tasted sweet, as if nature had added sugar to it.

"This water tastes so good," said Lillian.

"I know," said Katy. "Remember that summer we went to Yosemite? The water from the drinking fountain outside the Visitor Center tasted so good because it came from underground rivers deep inside the earth. This water tastes even better."

Maisy took a sip. "Tastes like tap water to me."

After they filled their bottles, they started walking again. Once they reached the top of the hill, they saw the moon and the mountains in the distance. It looked like a wall of glass separating day and night.

"Do we have to cross the mountains?" asked Katy.

"It's the only way," said Jack.

Jack and the girls walked until they stood at the place where day and night met. Lillian looked up. The wall ran as high as she could see, the sun on one side and the moon on the other.

"This should be impossible," she said.

"Let's go," said Jack as he stepped into the night. He turned and waited on the other side.

Katy stared at Jack. "This is so weird. You're in the night and we're in the day."

Jack saw that the girls looked scared. "It's just night," he said.

Maisy stepped up to the wall. "He's right. It's just night." She reached her hand through; the other side was much colder. Maisy shivered, then walked through. *I wish I had brought a jacket,* she thought.

Lillian and Katy looked at each other.

"It's OK," said Lillian. "I'll go first." She walked through the wall, turned, and smiled at Katy.

Katy walked up slowly. She moved her hand in and out of the darkness. *I guess it's OK,* she thought, and, closing her eyes, stepped through.

They climbed higher into the moonlit mountains. Katy stopped to look back at the foothills. She wished she could stay there, in the sun.

Rocks and boulders made it easier to climb. Every

few minutes Jack stopped, looked around, and then kept going. Sometimes he led them down a dead end and they had to go back and try a different way.

"You don't know your way around here," said Maisy.

"I live mostly in the forest and desert," said Jack.

"Great," muttered Maisy. "Do we have to cross a desert too?"

After walking for hours and not making much progress, Jack decided to stop and rest. He led them to a ring of tall, oddly-shaped boulders. They walked through a wide gap and stood in the center. The giant boulders surrounded them like a shelter.

"Let's rest a few hours," said Jack.

Maisy yawned. She and Lillian sat down near one of the boulders. "I should have brought a jacket," Maisy said, shivering.

Katy sat next to Jack. She pulled a small beach blanket from her pack and laid it on the ground. She took out her brush, mirror, and journal, then pulled a nut bar out of her backpack. "Are you hungry, Jack?"

Jack smiled and took the bar. "Thank you."

Katy opened a bag of dried fruit. She took a handful then passed the bag to Jack.

On the other side of the ring, Maisy nudged Lillian. She smirked and nodded toward Katy and Jack.

"Stop it," whispered Lillian.

Katy opened her water bottle. "Jack, how can you do all the amazing things you do?"

"He's only half human," said Maisy.

"Maisy," said Lillian. "Jack's not a monster."

"It's OK," said Jack. "Actually, in my world, humans are the monsters."

"Hey!" said Maisy.

Katy offered her water bottle to Jack. "But ... you're half human?"

"Actually," Jack began, "my mom is a siren, and my dad is a hippocamp—"

"A what?" laughed Maisy. "You're dad is a hippo?"

"A *hippocamp*," said Jack. "A hippocamp is a creature that lives in the ocean. His top half looks like a blue horse and his bottom half looks like a siren. All of the monsters had already been forced out of the world. But a few sea monsters, like hippocamps and sirens, stayed and hid in the deepest places.

"My mom loved land and human society. She could shape shift, so she transformed into a woman and moved to a small island. That's where I was born. My dad lived in the ocean around us.

"The island didn't get many tourists, and only a few families lived there. It had a town, a dock, a school, and a small forest. All the other kids went to school, so I explored the island every day. Most of it was wild and had lots of mammals, birds, reptiles, fish, and insects. Sometimes I'd catch marine iguanas or teach tropical birds to eat out of my hand. We lived there eight years. I loved all of the animals, but because I didn't go to school, I didn't have many friends. I was kind of lonely."

"Did you know you were different?" asked Katy.

"Sure," said Jack. "And I was afraid of the humans."

"*You're* afraid of *us?*" said Maisy. "You're the one with all the powers."

Lillian elbowed Maisy.

"Just look at your history," said Jack.

Maisy frowned and chewed her granola bar.

Jack took a sip of water. "More tourists started coming to the island. The beaches were too crowded for the iguanas, and the birds stopped eating out of my hand. Companies built houses and hotels. They chopped down the forest. The new docks were so crowded, I couldn't see the fish anymore. It was like an invasion. My mom went back to the ocean and I moved here."

Everyone sat quietly, lost in their own thoughts.

Maisy stood up. "Fine! I apologize for the whole human race! Humans are monsters! We're the bad guys!"

Everyone looked at each other, then laughed.

"What's so funny?" said Maisy. "I'm apologizing!"

Everyone laughed even harder. Maisy frowned, sat down and took another bite of her granola bar.

"Thank you, Maisy," said Jack. "You're the first human who has ever apologized to me."

For just a moment, Maisy blushed. "OK, OK, get on with your story."

Jack grinned. "I live here now, but I still visit my mom in the human world. One night, after the beach closed, I saw a girl standing on the jetty. That's how I met Bluebell. She had one of these."

He held up his medallion.

"Where did she get it?" Lillian wondered.

"We can talk more about this later," said Jack. "Let's get some rest. I'll take the first watch."

"Watch?" said Maisy. "Why do we need to watch?"

Jack stood up. "Well, this *is* a monster world and you *are* food."

"Thanks," grumbled Maisy, lying down. "Sweet dreams, everybody."

Chapter 19. A Shadow with Claws

It took a while for Lillian and Katy to fall asleep. They kept thinking about their parents. But the moment Maisy laid her head on the ground she was out like a light.

Jack listened to their quiet breathing as he looked up at the dark sky. *Was it a mistake to let Bluebell into our world?*

As Jack sat lost in thought, the full moon hung high in the starry sky. When he looked up two hours later, the moon stood in the same place, hovering over the snowy peaks. It was time to wake Katy.

To Katy, it seemed like only minutes had passed before Jack tapped her on the shoulder. She yawned and opened her backpack. She looked around to make sure no one was awake, then slid her fingers into a hidden pocket. She pulled out the little bronze key and unlocked her journal.

She opened the thick book and turned to a blank page. She reached into the backpack, pulled out a pencil, and wrote:

> *The adventure I didn't want to go on,*
> *the adventure I thought I'd hate,*
> *turned out to be better than I thought.*
> *I wish I was at home curled up in a blanket.*
> *But I enjoyed the parts of the adventure*
> *where we would sit and talk for awhile.*
> *I'm glad I met Jack, and if we didn't come here*
> *I wouldn't know him.*
> *Even though I'm afraid of the monsters,*
> *this world is beautiful.*

Katy read over her poem. She liked it, but her poems rarely came out right on the first draft. *OK,* she thought. *First, get rid of unnecessary words.*

> *The adventure I didn't want ~~to go on,~~*
> *~~the adventure I thought I'd hate,~~*
> *turned out to be better than I thought.*
> *I wish I was at home curled up in a blanket.*
> *But ~~I enjoyed the parts of the adventure~~*
> *~~where we would sit and talk for awhile.~~*
> *I'm glad I met Jack~~, and if we didn't come here~~*
> *~~I wouldn't know him.~~*
> *~~Even though~~ I'm afraid of the monsters,*
> *this world is beautiful.*

She read the poem again. *Better. Now, rewrite.*

*The adventure I didn't want
turned out to be better than I thought.*

*I wish I was at home curled up in a blanket,
but I'm glad I met Jack.*

*I'm afraid of monsters,
but this world is beautiful.*

She read it again. *Now* it felt perfect.

Katy spent the rest of her watch writing in her journal, but kept an eye on the night too. Soon it would be time to wake Maisy.

Maisy yawned. "Why do I have keep watch?" she grumbled to herself. "Katy should have woke Lillian first. There's nowhere anything could hide around here. It's just rocks and mountains."

The crags stood like shadows against the starry sky. She thought she saw a rocky peak move. She stared at the spot—three crags that looked strangely even. Maisy squinted then shook her head. *They're just crags.*

She yawned again and looked around. Everyone was asleep. She leaned back against a rock. *There's nothing here,* she thought. She closed her eyes and fell asleep.

High above, the three crags moved again, unfolding into huge wings.

The roc, a mythical bird of prey, leapt into the air. It was as big as a bus and had yellow, cat-like eyes and a dark brown beak that was as sharp as a ceramic knife.

Its wings blocked out the moon and hundreds of stars. Each sharp talon was nearly a foot long.

The roc scanned the circle of boulders. Jack and the girls looked as vulnerable as sleeping rabbits. The monstrous bird dove down, yellow eyes fixed on its prey.

An enormous shadow passed over Jack and the girls as they slept. The roc saw that it couldn't fit through the top of the ring. It flapped to stop from colliding into the boulders. The gust from its wings felt like a sudden whirlwind.

Everyone bolted awake, but before they could do anything one of the roc's giant claws reached into their camp and snatched Jack from the ground, bumping his head against a boulder.

"Jack!" Katy shrieked.

The roc flapped its huge wings. The wind blew the girls to the ground. They jumped to their feet and watched the roc turn into a shadow against the dark sky.

Katy spun on Maisy. "You were supposed to keep watch!"

"Yelling isn't going to help!" shouted Lillian.

"*You're* yelling!" shouted Maisy.

Lillian took a breath. "We need to do something."

"Yeah, we need to keep going," said Maisy. "We're on our own now."

Katy grabbed Maisy's shirt in her fist. "We have to help Jack!"

"You're insane," said Maisy as she peeled Katy's hand open. "He could be anywhere."

"We could climb in the direction the bird flew," suggested Lillian.

"I hate to be the one to say it," said Maisy, "but we're all thinking it. Jack is gone."

Katy shoved Maisy so hard that Maisy stumbled back, bumped into a boulder and slid to the ground. The look on Katy's face scared Maisy.

"We're *going*," declared Katy. She waited to see if anyone would say anything, then turned and marched out of the ring.

Lillian walked over and held out a hand to Maisy.

"Jack would have agreed with me," said Maisy as Lillian helped her up.

"I know," said Lillian. "But now it's not about Jack. It's about Katy."

Maisy and Lillian looked at each other.

"OK," whispered Maisy. She grabbed her metal bar and her backpack. She shook the weapon and grinned like her old self. "Let's go."

The roc beat its wings, flying higher and higher. Jack dangled, unconscious in the bony talons.

The mountains grew more jagged. Thousands of feet above, snowy peaks glistened in the moonlight.

The roc's aerie, made of trees uprooted from the forest, was nestled between two large crags. The roc hovered over the aerie, wings pounding the cold air. Its talons opened and Jack fell, tumbling, crashing into a treetop. The thin, dead branches broke his fall.

He rolled to the bottom of the nest, where he lay as still as death.

Squawk!

Jack slowly regained consciousness. His legs and ribs felt bruised.

Squaaawk!

He opened his eyes. Three baby rocs surrounded him. One perched on a branch above, one crouched on his right, and one inched closer on his left. Their gray, downy feathers made them look chubby and their big brown eyes were almost cute. They looked like baby eagles but were three times the size of Jack.

Snap! The bird on the right lunged. Jack dodged and the roc split the branch behind him. He ducked as the roc above went for his head. Jack jerked back, tripped over a root, and rolled out of the way just as the baby roc pounced down.

Jack looked around frantically. *There's no room to transform—*

One of the rocs jabbed at him. He rolled aside and sprung to his feet. All three birds pecked and lunged at the same time. Jack jumped, grabbed a branch and swung out of the way. One of the rocs leapt onto the branch above, snapping at his hands, forcing him to shuffle back and forth on the branch. Below him, the other two birds opened their mouths so wide they could swallow Jack whole. They bobbed under his feet, warbling hungrily.

The roc above snap-snap-snapped at Jack's hands, missing by just inches, chipping pieces out of the branch. Snap! It caught the edge of Jack's hand. He cried out and let go with one hand, dangling now closer to the rocs below. He swung his legs up as one of the rocs jumped, biting at his shoe. The other roc, thinking it was going to lose its food, pecked its sibling. The two birds fought, squawking loudly.

Jack knew this was his only chance. He let go of the branch and fell behind the fighting birds. He quickly squeezed between several tree trunks on the bottom of the nest as the roc above jumped down from its perch.

All three birds pecked wildly at Jack, but their beaks were too big to fit through the trunks and branches. He lay on his back, staring up at the hungry birds as they snapped at his face.

Jack pushed and squeezed under more branches. Below and off to the side was a small opening. As he climbed down, dead branches scraped his arms and face.

Finally, with a glance back at the baby rocs, who looked cute again as they whimpered over their lost food, Jack pulled himself through the gap. He grabbed a branch and hung under the nest, thousands of feet in the air. The foothills and the forest far below looked as small as a map.

Jack let go and fell into the abyss.

Chapter 20. The Griffin's Cave

While Jack fought for his life in the nest, the girls were running up the mountain, trying to find him. Katy led the way, but soon Maisy and Lillian had to rest.

"We need to keep moving," said Katy.

Maisy and Lillian were breathing so hard they couldn't answer.

"OK," said Katy. "But only for a few minutes."

Lillian dropped to the ground. Maisy flopped onto her back and Katy sat with her legs crossed. Lillian and Katy drank some water and shared a granola bar.

"Maisy, have some water," said Lillian.

"Later," huffed Maisy.

"You have to keep hydrated," said Katy.

"*Later,*" said Maisy.

Lillian sighed, then turned to Katy. "What are we

going to do when we find Jack and the bird?"

Katy thought about it. "I don't know."

"If we don't know," said Maisy, "why are we going at all?"

"Because it's the only thing we can do," said Katy.

Lillian took a sip of water. She looked up. "I can't get used to this. The moon in this sky." She turned and looked down toward the foothills. "The sun in that sky."

"I know," said Katy. She pointed at the stars. "The constellations are different too."

"Does that mean there's a universe inside our universe?" asked Lillian.

"Hey," said Maisy. "Still wondering how we're going to find Jack and that crazy bird?"

"Of course," said Lillian.

"We don't need to worry about finding the bird."

"Why?"

"Because *it* found *us*." Maisy sat up and pointed toward the peaks.

The roc glided into view, circling high above. It floated on outstretched wings, as motionless as a kite. Only its big head turned from side to side, scanning the ground.

The girls sprang to their feet. The motion caught the roc's eye. It banked into a dive.

Lillian looked for shelter and saw a cave about thirty yards down the mountain. "Come on!"

The girls ran. Every few steps, Katy looked back over her shoulder; each time, the roc was closer.

"We're not going to make it!" she shouted.

The girls ran faster. Only seconds away from the cave, a huge shadow swept over them. They ducked as the roc snatched at Lillian. The talons ripped her backpack open and knocked her into the cave. Maisy and Katy dashed into the dark opening and ran to her.

"Are you hurt?" asked Katy, helping Lillian to her feet.

"Just bruised, I think," said Lillian.

Maisy bent over with her hands on her knees, panting. "Look."

The roc crouched in front of the cave, extending its feathery neck to reach them, but its body wouldn't fit through the opening. It snapped at them in frustration.

"We'll never get out of here," said Katy.

The roc scratched at the ground, trying to push inside. Maisy bent down and picked up a big stone.

"Maisy …" warned Lillian.

But Maisy walked toward the monstrous bird and flung the stone. The bird blinked as the rock stuck right between its eyes.

"You scullion!" Maisy shouted, throwing more stones. "You rampallian! You fustilarian! I'll tickle your catastrophe!"

"Maisy!" said Lillian.

Maisy picked up a stone the size of a softball. She showed it to the bird in a teasing way, then thew with all her might. The stone hit the bird on the forehead. The roc gave a loud squawk that echoed through the cave. Lillian and Katy covered their ears.

"Stop, Maisy!" shouted Katy.

Maisy bent down and picked up two more stones, one in each hand. "I've had it with this world! Everything wants to kill us, capture us, or eat us! The metal monster, the stupid brownies, Medusa with her poison arrows, the crazy Kraken, the sirens, the chimera, those skeletal elves, more elves and more elves, and now this bird! And we never fight back! Well, I've had it! Let's show this big blue pigeon that we're not afraid!"

Katy and Lillian laughed.

"I'm not joking!" said Maisy. She tossed one stone to Lillian and the other to Katy.

Lillian caught the stone in both hands. Katy jumped back and let the stone hit the ground.

Lillian walked up and stood next to Maisy, who had already picked up another big stone. Maisy and Lillian looked at each other. Maisy nodded toward the bird, which was again trying to claw its way in.

Lillian threw. Thunk! The stone hit the bird on its beak.

Now Katy was standing next to Lillian. She threw a stone but only hit the wall of the cave.

Maisy turned to her. "How can you miss *that?*"

"Shut up," muttered Katy as she threw another stone, hitting the roc on its feathery blue head. "That's for Jack!"

The girls all pelted the bird with stones.

"Take that, you turkey!" said Maisy. "Thou zed! Thou unnecessary letter!"

Dirt flew as the roc tore at the ground, its talons ripping trenches into the earth. The bird banged its head on the walls, trying to force itself into the cave as stones struck over and over.

The bird screamed. It sounded so loud that the girls dropped their stones and covered their ears. In the silence that followed, they lowered their hands and stared at the furious roc.

"Think we made it mad?" grinned Maisy.

Before anyone could answer, they heard something behind them. They turned and stared into the dark of the cave. The noise grew louder.

"Sounds like a horse," said Katy, confused.

Katy was right. A big, four-footed creature was approaching out of the depths of the cave. They stared into the darkness, waiting.

Jack fell through the cold air. His short sleeves flapped and his shirt pressed against him. He felt like he was falling without getting closer to the ground.

He loved this feeling. He felt free. Everything lay spread out below him—mountains, foothills, and forest.

Jack stretched his arms wide. His nose and arms grew longer, his skin and clothing turned into bronze feathers, and his toes curled into sharp talons. In seconds, he was a hawk again.

The girls backed away from the darkness as the strange sounds grew louder, but could only go so far without coming within reach of the roc.

The noise grew louder and closer—then a big bird emerged out of the shadows, with a feathery, white head and a hooked beak. It looked like a giant bald eagle.

"Great," said Maisy. "Another monster bird."

The girls looked from the roc to the new bird. There was nowhere to go.

"We're trapped," said Katy.

"Out of the frying pan, into the fire," said Maisy.

But as the eagle walked out of the blackness, they saw that it wasn't an eagle at all.

"A griffin!" whispered Lillian.

The creature that stood before them was half eagle and half lion. It was twelve feet tall, and its white head tilted down, bronze eyes studying the girls. Dark brown feathers, with gold highlights on the edges, covered its shoulders and wings. Its front legs, layered with smaller feathers, ended in yellow, scaly feet and sharp talons. The rest of the griffin was a lion, its powerful muscles covered by smooth, tawny fur.

The griffin took a step forward. The girls flattened themselves against the wall, but the griffin walked right past them.

The griffin bent down, leaned toward the roc, and cawed a warning. The roc, twice the size of the griffin, screeched, pulled its head out of the cave, and hopped back as the griffin charged.

The girls ran to the mouth of the cave. The griffin and the roc stood in a stony clearing, staring at each other with their heads bobbing and bodies swaying from side to side.

"This isn't a fair fight," said Katy. "The griffin is so much smaller."

The roc lunged. The griffin hopped to the side. The roc snapped again. The griffin dodged so fast, it seemed to know what its enemy was thinking. It stabbed at the roc's shoulder, ripping out several long, blue feathers.

The roc shrieked angrily and rushed the griffin, its deadly beak biting the air. The griffin jumped back into a crouch, flapped its wings, and leapt over the roc, its lion paws kicking the roc's head. The roc screeched and launched into the sky.

The girls ran out of the cave. Already the mythical creatures were hundreds of feet above.

The roc chased the griffin through the night air, but the griffin swerved left and right. The roc was so much bigger that it made wider turns, falling farther and farther behind. The griffin flew straight up. The roc tried to follow, but the griffin, after hanging motionless, folded its wings and shot down like an arrow.

The roc tried to turn out of the way but it was too late. The griffin burst by, talons tearing at the roc's wing. Feathers flew into the air as the roc cried out in a high-pitched squawk. The roc tumbled downward, desperately trying to stay aloft, wings beating frantically.

Just before crashing into a crag, the roc regained its balance and flew away on a wounded wing.

The girls ran out and caught a big feather as it floated down. The three friends gathered around the surfboard-sized feather. It looked like it was woven of blue thread.

"Now I know how Alice felt in Wonderland," said Katy.

"Or Arrietty in The Borrowers," said Lillian.

"Or Ellie in Jurassic Park," said Maisy.

Chapter 21. Through the Mountain

The girls looked up. The griffin circled high above. He had been joined by a hawk about half his size. As they flew down, the girls recognized the hawk.

"Jack," whispered Katy.

The hawk hovered for a moment just above the ground, wings shrinking into arms, feathers becoming clothes and skin, talons becoming bare feet. And just like that, Jack was himself again.

Katy hugged him. "You're alive!"

Lillian put her arms around both of them, joining the hug. "How did you escape?"

Jack embraced Katy and Lillian. He felt his chest tighten and was surprised to find that he cared about these girls. About humans.

Lillian reached for Maisy to pull her in, but Maisy

stepped back and put up her hands.

"I'm happy he's alive too," she said. "But you know I don't hug."

Jack grinned. "Or stay awake."

"Yeah," said Maisy, looking uncomfortable. "Sorry about that."

"We should go," said a deep, noble voice.

Startled by the unfamiliar voice, the girls spun around. But they didn't see anyone except the griffin.

"This is Theron," said Jack. "Theron, these are my friends. Katy, Lillian, and Maisy."

"It is a pleasure to meet you, but we really should get inside," said the griffin in the same deep voice.

"You can talk?" said Lillian.

The griffin looked amused. "Everyone here can talk in their own way. Everyone in your world can talk too. In fact, whales have a better vocabulary than humans."

"He sounds like James Earl Jones in *The Lion King*," said Katy.

"Are you saying a dumb fish is smarter than me?" said Maisy.

Katy rolled her eyes at Lillian.

"We can continue this altercation later," said the griffin. He nodded his head toward the sky. "Unless of course you would like to discuss intelligence with the rocs."

Everyone looked up. A group of rocs flew against the night sky. One by one, they dove.

"Follow me," said the griffin.

He trotted into the cave, followed by Jack and the girls. Behind them, they heard the distant cries of rocs on the hunt.

The griffin led the way deeper into the cave. The light grew dimmer as they walked farther from the opening.

A sudden darkness fell. They felt wind rush in from behind, followed by flapping and earsplitting screeches. The girls turned around and covered their ears.

The mouth of the cave flashed with moonlight and shadow as the rocs fought to get in. The giant birds squawked and pecked at each other, but couldn't fit.

The air was cold. After the first turn, the light disappeared. They could barely see the griffin in front of them. Katy walked close to Jack, holding the edge of his sleeve. Lillian walked right next to the griffin. Maisy brought up the rear.

The cave began to feel like a maze. They turned right, then left, and came to several forks in the road. The griffin always knew which way to go, and always warned Jack and the girls before a steep decent.

"Is this a cave or a tunnel?" asked Lillian.

"The entire mountain range is full of tunnels," said the griffin. "We are in one of the main tunnels now. Smaller tunnels branch off, leading to dens where griffins make their homes. Our predators get lost in the maze and die, then we eat them."

"But the rocs are too big to get in," said Lillian.

"Rocs are not the only predators," said the griffin. "We are also hunted by wood elves and dog packs."

"Dogs aren't so bad," said Maisy.

"These dogs have three or more heads."

"Of course," said Maisy.

When they passed some of the smaller tunnels they heard distant fluttering or scratching. The noises sounded ghostly and far away.

Those must be the other griffins, thought Lillian.

The griffin turned and descended a steep slope. The girls saw tall flames dancing below. Small, colorful lights shone in the darkness all around the fire. As they walked closer, they saw that the lights were the glowing fruit they had first seen in the forest.

The tunnel ended in a huge cavern. Trees had been planted against the stony walls, neatly spaced five feet apart. The tops of all the branches spread into each other, while multicolored geometric fruit grew on the trunks. A pond filled one end of the cavern, the water a shimmering light blue. Strange fish swam close to the surface. Several huge nests, made of branches and covered with leaves and grass and feathers, surrounded the fire.

"Welcome to my den," said the griffin.

Lillian walked over to a tree and picked a square-shaped fruit, vertically striped green, red, blue, and purple. She also picked a circular fruit with a target pattern; the outer ring was yellow, the middle was purple, and the center dot was orange. Both pieces of fruit glowed in her hands like colorful nightlights.

"Can I sit here?" she asked, pointing at a nest.

"Of course," said the griffin politely. "Make yourself at home."

Lillian stepped into a big nest and sat down. The feathers and grass made it comfortable, but she could still feel the hard branches underneath.

She took a bite of the circle-shaped fruit. It crunched in her mouth and tasted like caramel and chocolate. "Mmmm," she hummed.

Maisy stepped into Lillian's nest with an armful of fruit. She plopped down and dropped the glowing fruit into their laps. *It looks like we're covered in Christmas lights,* thought Lillian with a smile.

Jack and Katy sat in the nest on the left. The griffin sat in the nest on the right and studied Lillian's face. "You are the one Jack was sent to find."

"Yes," said Lillian. "Bluebell is my sister."

"You two look so alike," said the griffin. "Ever since Bluebell came, things have changed. Out of the eighty wood elf tribes that live in the forest, most have joined under one command, forming an army. They now bring ropes when they hunt in our caves so they can find their way out. Even more unusual, the elves have learned to use paper and charcoal to draw maps of our mountain maze."

"What?" said Jack, looking up in surprise. "They don't even have a written language."

"Even worse, they are trying to catch *all* the dryads." The griffin looked down at his talons. "The elves brand the dryads and make them into slaves."

"We met a dryad in the elf prison," said Katy. "She helped us escape."

"But what does Bluebell have to do with any of this?" asked Lillian. She felt confused. Her fingers tightened around the fruit in her hands.

"I do not know for sure," said the griffin, deep in thought, "but I think she is helping some of the monsters start a war. That is why we sent Jack to find someone who knows Bluebell, someone who could help us talk to her."

A long silence followed. Everyone looked at Lillian.

"No," said Lillian. "I don't believe it."

"Think," said the griffin. "If you wanted to start a war, the first thing you would have to do is get the dryads under control. Whoever controls the dryads controls the trees and the forest."

"I don't know," said Jack.

"That is not all," said the griffin. "For the first time, rocs are moving their nests higher up … and dragon eggs are being stolen."

Jack's eyes widened. He looked like he had just heard the worst thing imaginable.

Katy put a hand on his arm. "What's wrong?"

"Dragon eggs are the most sacred thing in our world," said Jack. "It's more than a crime to steal a dragon egg. It's against nature."

"The kind of thing," said the griffin, "a human would do."

Everyone ate in silence. Lillian had lost her appetite.

"We have to find Bluebell," she said.

"The last I heard," said the griffin, "she was in the desert. We can go through the heart of the mountain. It is a day-long journey, so let us get a night of rest. You are safe here."

They all curled up to sleep. Everyone was so tired, they were asleep in minutes. Everyone but Lillian.

She lay propped up against the edge of the nest, wide awake, hands behind her head, gazing into the fire. The red and orange twisted and flickered restlessly, each flame wrestling the others, rising and falling, rising and falling.

After breakfast, the griffin guided them out of his den and back into the maze. The path led right and left, and unexpectedly slanted up and down. The darkness began to feel oppressive.

"Is there any light in here?" asked Lillian.

"I can make light if you wish," said the griffin.

Lillian stopped walking. "How can you *make* light?"

"Hold out your hands."

Lillian hesitated, then cupped her hands in front of her. Suddenly, a ball of red flame burst to life in her hands. She gasped and quickly dropped the fire. It floated gently down like an autumn leaf.

"Do not be afraid," said the griffin. "This is light, not fire."

Lillian exchanged glances with Maisy and Katy, then bent down and poked the blazing light with the tip of her index finger. The flames felt like thick air. She ran her fingers through the fluttering glow. It almost felt like moving her hand through water. She scooped up the ball of flames and stood. The light danced in her eyes.

Katy turned, cupped her hands, and held them out to the griffin. Instantly, her hands filled with flames.

"Me too!" said Maisy, reaching both hands toward the griffin. A rush of flame appeared in each hand. "This is awesome! I got two!" She juggled the light from one hand to the other.

"So beautiful," said Katy, moving her fingers through the flames.

Jack grinned at the griffin, who bowed his head.

"Put the lights on your head," said the griffin, "and you will be able to see."

The girls hesitantly placed the flames on their heads. It looked like they were wearing crowns of fire.

"I feel like a princess," said Katy.

"You look like a princess," said Jack.

Katy smiled and blushed.

Surrounded by light, Lillian felt her spirits rise. "Let's go," she said.

Now as they walked, they could see the rocky walls, the arched ceiling, and the tunnel curving ahead.

After walking several hours, they stopped for lunch, then continued their journey.

It seemed like they had been walking forever. Katy's feet hurt. Bored, Maisy was throwing the balls of flame into the air and trying to catch them on her head.

"Are we almost there?" she complained.

"Yes," said the griffin.

They turned a corner. Far ahead, they saw a little circle of daylight.

When they reached the mouth of the cave, the griffin stopped. The flames on top of their heads vanished.

"I will stay here tonight," he said. "I have much to do. But I will see you tomorrow."

"Thanks for helping us," said Lillian.

"My pleasure," said the griffin. "I hope I am wrong about your sister."

"Bye," said Katy.

"Can I take some of that fire with me?" asked Maisy.

The griffin almost seemed to laugh. With a bow to Jack, he turned and trotted back into the darkness.

As Jack and the girls stepped out of the tunnel, they felt like they had walked into an oven. The desert light blinded their eyes. At first all they could see was white. Slowly the world reappeared, but the only thing they saw was sand.

"You gotta be kidding me," said Maisy.

"Let's get out of this sun and heat," said Jack.

They camped in the mouth of the cave. Jack sat at

the entrance. "I'll keep watch."

Exhausted, Katy and Maisy fell asleep quickly. But Lillian, curled up on the ground, couldn't stop thinking about Bluebell. A memory drifted into her mind.

It was a bright, hot summer morning. Lillian was four and Bluebell was ten. Lillian heard footsteps running up the stairs. "Lillian!" called Bluebell as she entered the room, carrying a large book. "Look what I found in the garage!" Bluebell heaved the book onto the bed. The dark leather cover was gold-stamped with the words *Greek Myths.* Pictures of monsters surrounded the title. "What are grek mits?" asked Lillian. "Greek Myths," corrected Bluebell, smiling. "They're the best stories ever! Open it!" Lillian pulled the big book open. "What's that?" she asked, pointing at a three-headed dog. "That's Cerberus," said Bluebell. Excited, Lillian quickly turned the page. "Medasa?" she asked, trying to read the caption under the picture. Bluebell laughed. "Medusa." They went through the whole book that way, side by side.

The memory faded. *I forgot,* thought Lillian. *Bluebell was the one who introduced me to all those myths! She used to love them as much as I do. Apparently, she still does.*

That memory triggered another.

Lillian was eight and Bluebell was fourteen. It was spring and they were at the Beach of Green Waters. Lillian played in the sand, making castles. When Lillian looked up, Bluebell was sitting on the edge of the Crab Jetty, talking to a girl in the water. Suddenly, the girl dove under, and Lillian saw a pink tail splash the surface. She ran to the jetty but stopped because she was afraid of the crabs. "Bluebell!" she called. Bluebell walked back along the jetty, casually stepping around the crabs. "Bluebell!" Lillian shouted, bouncing up and down. "Were you were talking to a mermaid?!" Bluebell frowned and narrowed her eyes at Lillian. For the first time, Lillian felt afraid of her sister. "Mermaids are a myth," said Bluebell. "You were seeing things." Lillian walked back to her sand castles alone. After that day, Bluebell stopped reading the large book to Lillian.

Lillian felt more awake as the memories connected. She felt like she was putting a puzzle together. Bluebell, she realized, had known about this world all along. *And she never told me.*

Part Three

BATTLE

Chapter 22. Dragons in the Desert

Jack nudged Lillian awake. He held up a finger. "Shhh."

Scared, Lillian sat up and looked around. Everyone else was already awake.

Jack pointed outside. A big dog, twice as big as a Great Dane, sniffed around the sand. The dog turned toward the mouth of the cave. Now Lillian could see three ferocious, bristly heads.

"Cerberus!" she whispered.

The three-headed dog moved closer. It was about twenty yards away. One of its big heads looked right at them and growled. The other two heads turned. All three bared yellowed teeth.

"Move back into the cave," said Jack.

Maisy gripped her metal bar. Katy stared at Cerberus with wide eyes, too terrified to move. Lillian stumbled back, pulling Katy with her. Jack kept between the girls and the monstrous dog.

Cerberus reached the mouth of the cave. He could easily fit through the opening. He took a step inside— when a huge shadow passed over the sand.

All three heads looked up at the sky. Two heads growled and pulled toward Jack and the girls, while the third head whimpered and pulled away. The shadow passed over again. With a last growl and a snap, Cerberus turned and ran into the desert.

"Where's he going?" said Maisy.

Jack stepped out of the cave and looked up. "It's about time she got here."

"Who?" asked Lillian.

From high above they heard the flapping of massive wings. Wind and sand blew into the cave as the noise grew louder. The girls covered their eyes and stumbled back. After a few seconds the wind stopped. They opened their eyes and cautiously approached the mouth of the cave. At first, all they saw was a cloud of dust.

But as the sand settled, they saw a light blue dragon towering over them.

Each of the dragon's scales were ice blue with dark blue edges. This made the dragon look like she was wearing ocean waves. Her friendly, intelligent eyes looked like shiny, dark blue pearls.

Jack stood by the dragon. He only came up to her knee. "This is Nevara," he said. "Nevara, these are my friends. Lillian, Katy, and Maisy."

The girls stayed in the mouth of the cave, staring at the dragon. Lillian came out first.

The dragon bowed. "Pleased to meet you."

"Dragons are real!" said Lillian. She was so excited to see one of her favorite myths in real life, she walked right up to Nevara and touched the blue scales. The tough skin felt like she imagined a crocodile might feel. "This is like a dream come true. You feel as cool as snow."

"I'm a frost dragon," said Nevara. "I live high in the mountains."

Katy walked toward the dragon. "Amazing." She stroked Nevara's rough, wintry scales.

"Can you breathe ice?" asked Maisy.

"Of course," said Nevara.

"Prove it," said Maisy.

"I can put you into an ice block," said Nevara.

"You can show us later," said Maisy.

Nevara laughed and bent her head down toward Jack. "I had forgotten that some humans can be funny."

Lillian and Katy grinned at Maisy, who frowned.

"The griffin told me you need a ride," said Nevara. She bent down low, her head almost touching the ground. Jack jumped twelve feet into the air and landed on Nevara's back.

"Climb up the tail," he called.

The girls hesitated.

Lillian smiled at the long, serpentine tail. "Climb a dragon's tail?"

"Go on," said Nevara. "Unless you'd rather walk through the desert."

The girls walked up the tail. The dragon's flesh bent under their feet and the scales pushed into the soles of their shoes like sharp stones. In no time, they were sitting behind Jack.

"Hold on," he said. "You're going to love this."

Nevara flapped her powerful wings and rose into the air. Excited and scared, the girls gripped under the large scales with the tips of their fingers, desperate to hold on.

Nevara soared through the desert. The wind blew the girls' hair like a blow dryer. They felt exhilarated as the dragon bobbed up and down, smooth as a merry-go-round. The girls squinted into the hot, gusting air.

"This is awesome!" shouted Maisy.

On either side, the huge wings rose and fell. The bony ridges were dark blue with light, frosty blue flaps of skin stretched between.

The mountains grew smaller behind them. Soon, all they could see was sand.

I wonder why Bluebell chose the desert, thought Lillian as she stared out at the endless yellow sea. *How can anything survive here?*

After riding for hours, the exhilaration had worn off. Everyone's legs felt stiff from straddling the dragon's back. Their eyes stung from the dry wind and their faces felt sunburned.

"This isn't so awesome," said Maisy.

In the distance, Lillian saw a speck of green. *Is that a cactus?* she wondered. As they flew closer, the cactus grew bigger and bigger. Now she could see there were five dome-shaped cacti surrounding one in the center. It was the size of a small town.

As they flew closer, Lillian saw dragons sitting on top of each dome. The dragon on the center dome was red and orange, like fire. The dragons on the smaller domes were green, blue, brown, yellow, and black. They looked like they were keeping guard over a treasure.

The girls stared at this amazing dragon haven. Suddenly, Nevara dove into an opening in the main cactus dome. The girls held on as they dropped into cool shade.

The inside of the cactus was hollow, rounded, and as open as the Taj Mahal. Dragons of different sizes and colors filled the space—flying, sitting, talking, or sleeping. They looked like they came from the mountains and forests, deserts and caves, and brought the air of those places with them.

"Smells like Yosemite," said Lillian.

"Looks like a dog park for dragons," said Maisy.

Nevara landed between a green forest dragon and a black night dragon. Both dragons looked at the girls with suspicion and loathing.

"They don't like us," Katy whispered to Lillian.

Jack and the girls slid off Nevara's back.

"Don't worry," said Nevara. "The other dragons won't hurt you if you're with me."

"Where have I heard that before?" said Maisy.

The girls stared at the dragons around them. One orange and red dragon had horns that curled like a ram's; smoke came out of its slit-thin nostrils. Another dragon had a flat face with enormous multi-colored eyes and translucent, rainbow-colored scales. A long-necked dragon had scales as green as leaves, with a bristly tail that looked like it was made out of thorny branches. A tiny blue dragon, the size of a cat, looked like living frost; the spikes on its head and tail were like icicles that never melted.

Everywhere they looked they saw a different kind of dragon. No two dragons in the entire room looked the same.

"For years I've imagined a world of dragons," said Lillian. "This is even better."

Nevara led Jack and the girls down a hallway and into a small room. Light streamed inside through a square opening in the domed ceiling.

"This is where you'll sleep," said Nevara. "Is there anything you'd like to know before I leave?"

Maisy and Katy sat on the soft, spongy floor. But Lillian took a step forward. "Is it true a war is coming?"

"The griffin already told you?" asked Nevara.

Lillian nodded. "But I don't believe him. Bluebell wouldn't help start a war."

Nevara sighed and sat down. "It's a long story."

Lillian sat next to the dragon. "I want to know." Her hair, shoulder-length since their encounter with Medusa, was tangled and uncombed. Her olive skin was dirty and sunburned, but a frightened determination shone through. "I *need* to know."

Nevara's blue eyes filled with sadness. "Some of the monsters have wanted to take back the human world for a long time. The leaders of the wood elves, desert trolls, and mermaids have been working on this for centuries. They wanted a human to join them. Someone to teach them to be truly ruthless.

"For hundreds of years, the mermaids went back and forth between the worlds, searching for the right human. They found Bluebell when she was four years old. We don't know why they chose your sister, but they must have seen something in her because they've been mentoring her ever since, telling her stories about the first war, filling her with promises and plans to get the earth back.

"Then something must have happened, because two years ago Bluebell moved here. Since then, things have changed in Lanodeka."

"I still don't believe Bluebell is involved," said Lillian. "You have no proof."

Nevara looked deeply into Lillian's eyes. "Bluebell asked the dragons and griffins to join her army, but we said no. I was there."

Lillian hunched against the soft wall. She looked

down at her shoes as she crumbled from the inside out. *Bluebell, what are you doing?*

"Dragons and griffins don't believe in revenge," said Nevara. "Bluebell was angry. She swore a war was coming. She spoke for the mermaids, trolls, elves, orcs, and many others. It was her idea to steal our eggs, to raise dragons to fight on their side. She said nothing could stop them. She spoke of new magic and new weapons. Then she found out *you* had entered the world."

Nevara waited until Lillian looked up.

"She really knows I'm here?" asked Lillian.

Nevara nodded. "She sent the chimera to bring you to her, but the chimera was caught by the elves. He told us that a human saved him and now he and all his kind are on our side. So Bluebell sent that three-headed dog to find you."

Lillian felt more frightened than ever. "What does she want from me?"

"To join her, of course."

"So," said Jack in a somber voice, "a civil war is coming to Lanodeka?"

Nevara shook her head. "It's already here. Griffins are arriving late tonight. We go to battle in the morning."

Chapter 23. Finding Bluebell

Jack had gone back to the main room with Nevara. He wanted the girls to decide for themselves what they were going to do.

"Jack thinks we should leave this world now," said Katy. "I think so too. If we fight, we could die. We might even have to kill someone."

Lillian nodded, all tangled inside, feeling sadness, surprise, and anger all at the same time. "Maybe we should turn back. Maybe there's no point in going on. I came all this way to find Bluebell. I thought she was lost and alone. But she ran away to this place. She chose to be here. And now she's involved in a war. This is all so crazy."

"So we're leaving?" asked Katy hopefully. "Maybe we can talk Jack into coming with us."

"I don't know," said Lillian. "You should leave. I mean it. I don't want either one of you to get hurt. But for me, if I leave, I'll regret it for the rest of my life. I have to at least try to talk to Bluebell. She might not listen to anyone else. What if I can help stop this war? Don't I have a responsibility to try? We're talking about a war between two worlds."

"Why are we talking about this at all?" said Maisy. "We're kids! We shouldn't be going to war! I'm out."

Katy put her hand on Lillian's shoulder. "I have to agree with Maisy. We're just kids. We should go home. Our parents must be going crazy."

Home. Lillian wished she *could* go home. But she knew she couldn't.

Finally, after a long silence, Lillian said, "I can't." She leaned forward and hugged Katy tight. "Bye," she whispered. "Take care of Maisy on the way back."

Katy's eyes filled with tears, but before she could say anything, Lillian turned to Maisy and forced her into a tight hug. "Bye—" Lillian started.

Maisy pushed her away. "What are you talking about?"

"We're not leaving you," said Katy.

"We're in this stupid adventure together," said Maisy.

"You have to go," said Lillian. "It's too dangerous—"

"Shut up, Lillian," said Katy with a small smile. She grabbed Lillian and hugged her with all her might. Suddenly Katy and Lillian were both crying.

Maisy rolled her eyes. "Keep that up and I *will* leave."

Lillian reached out but Maisy stepped back. "How many times do I have to tell you? I do not hug."

Lillian and Katy laughed and wiped their tears.

That night, Lillian couldn't sleep. She couldn't stop thinking of her sister. *Does Bluebell really believe that monsters should rule the world? Would she really betray her own kind? Would she really start a war?*

Memories she had forgotten began to rise like a tide. She remembered one summer day when she was eight. Bluebell had taken Lillian, Katy, and Maisy to the park. Bluebell sat on a bench while the younger girls played. They took off their shoes and climbed a tree. The trunk bent almost horizontal to the grass, so even Katy could climb it. A bee crawled on the bark, and Katy accidentally stepped on it. She screamed, grabbed her foot, lost her balance, and fell backwards off the tree. She landed flat on her back and lay stunned, the breath knocked out of her body. A moment later, Katy started to cry. "Bluebell!" called Lillian as she rushed over to Katy. Bluebell stood up and walked toward the girls. Maisy hopped out of the tree while Lillian helped get the stinger out of Katy's foot. "Bluebell!" shouted Maisy. "Katy's been stung!" But Bluebell walked right past them. She bent down in the dirt and gently picked up the bee. "What about Katy?" said Maisy. Bluebell ignored her. She touched the bee's broken wings. "You killed it," she said, walking away with the bee in her hand. It was as if the bee meant more to her than Katy.

Another memory swept across her mind. Lillian was nine. She and Bluebell had spent the day at the zoo. The afternoon was so gray and cloudy that you could hardly see the sun. It began to drizzle. Most visitors had left; all the animals were in their dens so there wasn't much to see. Bluebell led Lillian straight to the Reptile House. It was so silent inside they could hear the snakes hissing behind the glass. The black mamba turned as Lillian passed. Corn snakes, rattlesnakes and boa constrictors lay curled in sleep. Lillian stopped to look at the beautiful eastern coral snake. Bluebell pointed at the next cage. "Look," she said. "A Komodo dragon." Lillian stared at the huge lizard. It stared right back but didn't move, except for its long black tongue, which flicked in and out. It was bigger that she was. "Don't you feel sorry for him?" asked Bluebell. "That amazing reptile cooped up in that little cage? Isn't it terrible what humans do to creatures like this?" "Yeah," said Lillian. "I wish they could just live in their natural habitat." "Would you really like to see him free?" asked Bluebell. Lillian nodded. Bluebell reached to the door at the edge of the glass cage. She pushed down on the handle, pulled the door toward her, and held it open. "How did you do that?" asked Lillian, suddenly scared. Bluebell shrugged. "Maybe they forgot to lock the door." Lillian stared in horror as two Komodo dragons walked through the door like dinosaurs. The dragons looked up at Bluebell as if asking her something, then walked right past the girls and disappeared into the zoo. A few seconds later, Lillian heard screaming. Bluebell grabbed Lillian's hand and rushed out of the zoo, never letting go until they got home. Lillian told her parents what had happened, and Bluebell got in trouble. Bluebell called Lillian "traitor" for weeks.

Then a more recent memory rolled across her mind.

Lillian was ten. She climbed through her window into the tree and sat on one of the higher branches, munching sweet mulberries. Her fingers were stained purple from the juice of the long, bumpy fruit. The bark was rough but Lillian didn't mind. She climbed deeper into the tree. Looking through a gap in the branches, she saw Bluebell's bedroom. Curious, Lillian peered inside. The room was painted purple. A bed with a blue blanket stood in the corner, and four small cupboards and three cubbies lined the walls. Then Bluebell walked in quickly and shut the door. Outside the window, Lillian leaned back and pulled two branches in front of her face. She peeked through the leaves and saw Bluebell drop a round stone on the bed. The stone glowed red, the light hitting the ceiling and walls. Lillian stared at it, wondering what it could be. If only she could get a closer look. But Bluebell reached into a cubby, grabbed a sock, slipped the stone inside, and pushed it to the bottom of her beach bag. That was the day Bluebell had disappeared.

Lillian felt like she was in a tsunami of memories. She now realized that she barely knew her sister. She felt like a weight was pressing down on her heart.

She looked across at Katy and Maisy. Katy was wide awake too. They exchanged worried smiles as Maisy slept, snoring as peacefully as if she were at home.

The next morning, Nevara led Jack and the girls to an opening in the cactus wall overlooking the desert. The girls stared in awe at hundreds of griffins, chimeras, and dragons who had gathered for battle. The chimeras all looked the same, and so did the griffins. But the dragons were all different colors and sizes. Some were as small as bats and others were larger than whales.

"This is the most amazing thing I've seen in my entire life," said Lillian.

"Yeah," said Maisy. "Too bad we're all about to die."

"That's not funny," said Katy.

The girls heard a "Baaa" behind them. They turned to see Fred the chimera, Theron the griffin, and a dragon the size of a pony, its scales as green as leaves.

"Fred!" shouted Katy. The chimera purred as she stroked its mane.

"It's so nice to see you again, Theron," said Lillian to the griffin.

Theron bowed. "It is a great pleasure to see you as well, Lillian."

Maisy stepped up to the dragon. "What's your name?"

"Zoe," said the dragon. Her voice sounded low, like wind through summer leaves. "I'm a forest dragon."

"I'm a … city human," said Maisy.

Everyone laughed.

"What?" said Maisy, turning to Lillian and Katy. Lillian just smiled and shook her head.

Nevara turned to Fred, Zoe, and Theron. "Protect the humans. If you see a chance to get Lillian to Bluebell, take it. Otherwise, keep them out of the battle."

The creatures nodded.

Nevara looked at the girls. "Even though you're not going to fight, I have weapons if you want to defend yourselves."

Jack knelt by a leather bundle. He untied the knot and unfolded the sides, revealing a stash of ancient weapons: swords, spears, bows and arrows, and shields.

Katy picked up a bow and quiver of arrows. The bow was plain wood and about four feet tall.

"Are you sure?" said Lillian.

"I want to be able to protect us if things get really bad," said Katy. "And this is perfect."

She lifted the strap of the quiver over her head and across her chest. She plucked the bowstring with her finger. It was tighter than the bow she had at home, but she felt confident all the same.

"Where did you get these?" she asked.

"We built a museum," said Jack, "where we keep things from the first war. They're enchanted to preserve them over time."

Maisy picked up a sword belt and short sheath. She fastened the belt around her waist and pulled out the sharp sword. It was so heavy that she needed both hands to lift it over her head.

"This would be awesome," said Maisy, "if we weren't about to die."

Lillian looked through the stash and found a small, round shield. Bits of white paint remained from the original design, but the symbol had been hacked off. On the back were two straps for her arm. She tried it on. It fit perfectly.

"Is everyone ready?" asked Nevara.

The girls exchanged glances.

"Ready as we'll ever be," said Lillian.

They flew across the dessert. Lillian held on tight as hot wind tousled her hair. Dragons and griffins sailed all around her. It looked like the whole desert was made out of mythical creatures. She felt amazed and scared at the same time. *Am I really in a world with monsters, riding on a dragon, going into battle against my own sister, with only a shield to protect myself? Is this really happening?*

Lillian looked to her left and saw Maisy flying Zoe, the forest dragon. Maisy turned, smiled, and shook her sword in the air.

OK, thought Lillian. *This is really happening.*

She gazed down at hundreds of chimeras below. They ran under the dragons and griffins like a wild shadow. Katy rode on Fred in the middle of the pack. She looked up and waved.

Lillian took a deep breath, then looked around at the vast sweep of dragons and griffins. She squinted at the horizon where the colorless sky met the pale yellow sand, wondering what would happen when she finally met her sister.

Up ahead, the desert ended in a cliff. The sand stopped at a rocky ledge. Beyond that, Lillian saw a wall of clouds—and nothing else. *Looks like the end of the world.*

No army. No battle. Just sand and cliffs and clouds. The griffins and dragons looked as confused as Lillian.

But as they slowly descended, Lillian realized the desert wasn't completely empty. There was one person waiting near the edge of the cliff.

"Bluebell," whispered Lillian.

Chapter 24. The Stone

Lillian, riding the griffin, along with Jack and Maisy riding dragons, glided down and landed on the sand fifty feet from Bluebell. The other dragons and griffins circled above, keeping watch. Past the cliffs, the thick clouds stood like a wall.

Lillian slid off Theron and started running to Bluebell. But someone grabbed her arm. She turned and saw Jack.

"Be careful," he said. "This has to be a trap. Bluebell's army must be nearby or she wouldn't be here alone."

Lillian nodded and walked across the sand toward Bluebell. Her sister wore dragon-hide shoes, tawny leather pants, and a white, furry shirt with snakeskin straps. In the two years she had been gone, her red curly hair had grown almost to her elbows. Her face looked weathered and her green eyes shone with determination. She looked so much older than eighteen.

Lillian felt sadness, confusion, happiness, anger and disappointment, all wrestling inside of her. But then, through all that, came the strongest emotion of all—love. Her eyes filled with tears as she threw her arms around her sister.

"I found you!" she whispered.

Bluebell didn't hug Lillian back, but gently pushed her away. "You look so different," she smiled sadly. She ran her fingers through Lillian's hair. "You cut your hair."

Lillian wiped away her tears. "Actually, that was Medusa. And you're not wearing all that blue eye shadow." She touched her sister's face. "What are you doing here, Bluebell?"

"I could ask the same of you," said Bluebell. "Ever since I heard you were here, I've been trying to find you. I have permission to invite you to join us. If you stay with the dragons and griffins, you'll lose this war. You may even die. If you join me, we could free this world *and* the human world."

Lillian was about to answer when she noticed the medallion around Bluebell's neck. It looked exactly like the one Jack wore.

"Where did you get that?"

"It belonged to mom," said Bluebell. "I stole it. That's how I got in."

Lillian shook her head. "Mom? I don't understand any of this."

"Just think of it like one of your Harryhausen movies," said Bluebell. "Like *Clash of the Titans,* but in this story the monsters are the good guys."

Bluebell reached into a pocket and pulled out a shining red stone. Lillian recognized the stone she had seen through the bedroom window. Bluebell handed it to her.

As soon as Lillian's fingers closed around the glowing stone, images burst in her mind: dragons glided through the Grand Canyon; rocs built nests on Half Dome; dryads spoke to trees in the South American rain forest; mermaids in the clear Caribbean sea followed a siren with red hair; three-headed dogs prowled the Sahara; frost dragons hunted in the Himalayas; elves built forts in redwood forests; brownies dug tunnels on the prairies; griffins lived in caves around Ayers Rock.

The images gave Lillian a feeling so peaceful and beautiful that she wanted to be part of it. But suddenly the images changed: humans in boats harpooned mermaids as the red-haired siren squirmed out of a net and dove deep; rocs were shot down by armies of archers; soldiers with spears attacked and killed chimeras; elves ran as forests burned around them; dragons were impaled by massive crossbows; griffins were battered by catapults; wounded monsters sat in prisons and zoos.

Under the spell of the stone, Lillian felt like these things were happening to *her.* The pain made her drop to her knees.

Again the images changed: monsters hid from humans in caves; mythical animals tunneled deep underground; magical creatures migrated out of the human world; the red-haired siren waved to a dryad who then disappeared into a tunnel; the siren dove underwater, her red hair flowing behind, her face becoming more familiar as she swam closer.

Mom! thought Lillian.

She dropped the stone. The world around her faded back into view. Katy, Maisy, and Jack rushed to her, but Bluebell helped her up first.

"Understand now?" said Bluebell. "You belong here as much as I do."

"Are you OK?" asked Katy.

"What happened?" said Maisy, glancing at Bluebell.

Lillian was still dazed from the images. *Mom!*

"Join me," said Bluebell, as she picked up the stone and put it in her pocket.

"You want me to help start a war?" asked Lillian.

"It's the only way," said Bluebell. "Trust me, there's more going on here than you realize."

Lillian took a small step back. "Can't we talk to the humans and make an agreement? No one has to die."

Bluebell shook her head. "Look at human history, Lillian. They drove us out by force. They'll never share what they stole. I don't want anyone to die either. But sometimes you have to make sacrifices. We have to *take* the world back."

"I agree the humans were wrong. But to steal the world back isn't right, either."

Bluebell pointed an accusing finger at her sister. "But it *is* right! This is *justice*, Lillian! Join us and you guarantee the safety of mom, dad, Katy, Maisy, and yourself. Stay with them," she gestured rudely at Jack, "and you'll all die."

Lillian's voice faltered. "Mom and dad?"

"Maisy and Katy?" Maisy interjected.

Bluebell stepped up and put a hand gently on Lillian's shoulder. "This is war. Please. Join me."

Lillian's hazel-green eyes shone with desperate hope. "That's why I *can't* join you. This *is* war. A war between two worlds. You know what kind of weapons the humans have. Weapons that can destroy *all* of this. The monsters only have their natural powers and magic. But what kind of magic can stand against bombs? Millions of people and creatures will die. Even if you win, both worlds could be destroyed."

She held Bluebell's face in her hands. "Please, stop this war before it's too late."

For the first time Lillian saw doubt in her sister's eyes. But then Bluebell slowly stepped back, leaving Lillian's hands holding empty air.

"Goodbye, Lillian," she whispered.

Behind Bluebell, the clouds began to stir. The girls heard a deep rumbling and the ground shook like a small earthquake.

Jack and the girls watched in terror as thousands of rocs flew out of the clouds. They were different colors, depending on their size. The smallest ones, the size of rhinos, were a dirty, brownish red; others, the size of semi-trucks, were a dark, grimy blue; the largest rocs, as big as flying houses, were black as basements.

The girls backed into Nevara and Zoe as the deadly storm of rocs flew overhead. Dragons, griffins, and rocs slashed and ripped at each other with sharp talons, and struck and jabbed and bit with their beaks and teeth. Looking up, Lillian felt like she was in a summer blockbuster she didn't want to see.

After the rocs passed by, a swarm of dark birds flew through the clouds.

"Are those crows?" asked Lillian.

"Worse," said Jack. "Harpies."

The harpies had the bodies of vultures, with the heads, necks, and arms of women. They had gray, reptilian skin and huge, black raptor eyes. Instead of hair they had feathers. Each finger ended in a long talon. Sharp, venomous fangs hung down past their chins.

The girls were still focused on the battle above when they heard a high-pitched wailing. They turned in time to see a white wave of wood elves spill over the edge of the cliff.

"This is bad," said Jack. "There shouldn't be this many. They have most of Lanodeka on their side."

Over the pandemonium of the battle in the sky and the yelling of elves, they now heard a low roar as a surge of orcs climbed over the cliff. The orcs were corpse-gray and looked like carcasses sown together. They carried axes, clubs, stone hammers, and crude maces. Goblins streamed after the orcs, screaming a loud battle cry. The goblins were taller than the elves and had pointy ears and green skin. After the goblins, creatures Lillian had never seen, even in books or movies, swept over the cliff in tides.

Shrieking filled the sky. The girls looked up. Thousands of winged creatures chased each other through the hot air, cawing and roaring and clawing and tearing. Blasts of dragon fire lit up the rocs like torches; frost dragons froze harpies with icy breath. Scores of rocs dug their talons into dragons the size of passenger planes, forcing them down, eating as they fell.

A huge roc, engulfed by flames, exploded into the sand just yards away from Jack and the girls. Burning hot sand hit their arms and faces. As they stumbled back, they heard blood-curdling screams from above. Two harpies dove down, claws extended. Fred leapt and ripped the harpies out of the air, crushing them to the ground.

More rocs and dragons were falling out of the sky. Elves with spears and nets caught and killed griffins. Chimeras feasted on orcs and brownies. Other griffins flew close to the ground, snatching goblins and hurling them high into the air.

"Run!" Jack shouted to the girls, but they couldn't hear anything over the chaos of the battle.

Lillian tripped as a brownie grabbed her leg. Maisy kicked it and it went flying through the air like a stone.

"Run!" Jack cupped his hands to his mouth. "Run!" But the girls kept tripping over the brownies that scurried all around their feet.

Jack jumped onto Nevara. Zoe landed next to them. They turned around to face a large pack of elves. Nevara froze several with her icy blue breath but the others charged. In an instant, Jack and the two dragons were surrounded.

Meanwhile, Fred the chimera and Theron the griffin fought a group of orcs, driving them away from the girls.

An orc slipped by Fred and charged right at Lillian. She swung her shield in front of her face. The orc's club hit her shield with such force that it knocked Lillian to the ground. She peered over her dented shield as the orc lifted its club—when an arrow sunk into its head. It staggered backwards and fell to the ground.

Lillian looked and saw Katy holding her bow.

"I didn't mean to kill him!" stammered Katy, trembling.

Maisy helped Lillian to her feet. "We gotta get out of here!"

Spotting the girls, a group of goblins sped in from behind. The girls ran, stumbling over the swarming brownies. Every time Katy looked over her shoulder, the goblins were closer. One of them threw a weighted net over Katy. She screamed and fell, pinned to the sand. Lillian and Maisy ran back to help. As they tried to pull Katy out of the net, a loud roar shook the air.

Fred the chimera leapt in front of Katy. It ripped off one goblin's head and fought the others while Lillian and Maisy freed Katy from the net.

One of the goblins ducked under Fred's paw. Maisy turned to it and pulled her sword out of its sheath. Using both hands, she lifted the sword above her head and struck awkwardly. The goblin leaned back with a smirk and the blade missed its body completely— but stuck into its foot. The goblin screamed, spraying Maisy with its vile spit. As Maisy tried to pull the sword out, she saw the goblin grab a knife out of its belt. Maisy let go of the sword and punched as hard as she could. The goblin fell onto its back.

Zoe and Theron joined Fred, scaring away the goblins for a few seconds. Lillian helped Katy onto Fred as Maisy pulled herself up onto Theron's back. Lillian climbed onto Zoe, hoping they could all get away. But as her arms reached around Zoe's neck, the dragon's green scales grew cold and gray. In a instant, Zoe had turned to stone.

Lillian looked up—and saw Medusa slithering through the orcs.

Chapter 25. Lillian's Burden

Lillian watched as Medusa slithered toward them—then remembered not to make eye contact. But Medusa wasn't looking at her. Jack, sitting on Nevara's back as she tried to break free from a pack of orcs, was Medusa's next target.

"Jack!" Lillian shouted. "Jack! Medusa's behind you!"

But he had already seen Medusa. He slid off Nevara as Medusa nocked an arrow. Jack put up both hands. A clear divider formed between him and Medusa like a wall of water. Medusa released the arrow. It curved off course as it went through the wall, missing Jack completely. Medusa grimaced.

Nevara turned to help when a large net fell across her. Before she could shake it off, another net covered her head. Elves ran in two groups on either side. They kept trying to hammer the net into the ground using wood stakes. The net's magic prevented Nevara from breathing ice. She roared and tried to blast the elves, but only a chilly fog came out of her mouth.

"We have to help Jack!" shouted Katy. The girls could barely hear her over the din. Katy drew an arrow, nocked it, and aimed at Medusa. Her hands trembled. *What if I miss? She'll turn us to stone!*

She was about to release the shaky arrow when Lillian stepped close and put a hand on her arm.

"I have a better idea," said Lillian. She picked up one end of the net and pointed at Medusa. Katy nodded and grabbed the other side while Maisy, grinning, lifted the back. Together, they snuck up behind the gorgon.

This time, Medusa aimed slightly to the side, so the arrow would curve and hit Jack right in the head. But as she aimed, Jack made the wall thicker. With a scowl, Medusa released the poisoned arrow, but the shaft moved through the barrier as if in slow motion. It stopped halfway through, suspended in the clear, viscous wall.

Jack made the wall even thicker as an elf pack joined Medusa. Their smaller arrows all embedded into the wall. More elves joined the fight, but still, their arrows and spears couldn't penetrate. Jack spun, hands raised, as another pack of screaming elves appeared to his right.

Now Medusa had a clear shot.

She nocked an arrow, aiming at Jack's heart. He saw her out of the corner of his eye.

Medusa released the arrow.

Jack whipped around, caught the shaft right in front of his chest, and dove to the ground as the elves released a volley of arrows over his head. The arrows hit the elves who were tying Nevara to the ground. Nevara shook off the net and blasted the elves with ice.

At that moment, the girls thrust the magic net over Medusa and pulled her to the ground.

"Close your eyes ... and don't let go!" shouted Lillian.

Too late! As Maisy pulled the net tight, she looked directly into Medusa's yellow snake eyes.

"Maisy!" shouted Katy.

Maisy froze. *What a stupid way to die!* she thought. But she didn't turn to stone.

Lillian laughed. "The magic net! She has no power!"

Maisy let go of the net and waved her hands. "I can move? I'm alive?"

Medusa started to lift Maisy's side of the net.

"Maisy!" yelled Lillian.

Maisy grabbed the net again and held it down. Medusa writhed in the sand, trying to break free. The gorgon let out a gurgling hiss, her snake-like tongue flicking in and out of her mouth. Maisy tightened her grip. "Out of my sight! Thou dost infect my eyes!"

Jack ran up, carrying the stakes from the frozen elves. Together they hammered the net deep into the sand.

Maisy reached through one of the holes and touched Medusa's scaly skin.

"There," she said. "I touched Medusa."

Other dragons landed next to Nevara and helped clear a small space.

"We can't win," said Jack. "There are too many."

Lillian's eyes filled with tears as she gazed at the destruction all around her. Jack was right. Dead creatures lay everywhere on the sand. Some, liked Zoe, had been turned to stone. Others were just charred shapes from dragon fire. Hundreds of creatures were caught under nets, wounded by arrows or impaled by spears.

Lillian looked across the battlefield at Bluebell. Now other monsters stood with her—a goblin, an orc, a troll, and a wood elf. *Those must be the other leaders,* thought Lillian.

Behind the leaders, more and more creatures swarmed over the cliff like an endless wave of war.

"We lost," said Jack. He jumped onto Nevara. "We have to retreat."

The dragons, griffins, and chimeras that were still alive followed Jack and Nevara. Lillian flew on Theron, and Maisy on a big, black dragon. Katy rode Fred below them, followed by the surviving chimeras. Thousands of rocs, harpies, orcs, goblins, elves, and trolls chased after them, catching the slow and wounded.

Finally, the pursuing waves pulled back into a shouting and cheering sea.

Lillian looked over her shoulder. Bluebell grew smaller and smaller. Lillian didn't look away until Bluebell had completely disappeared.

As they crossed the desert, many of the dragons, griffins, and chimeras went home to the mountains, caves, and forests. The rest made their way toward the cactus haven.

As they flew, Lillian cried into Theron's feathers.

Inside the cactus, Jack left the girls in a small chamber while he talked with Nevara and the other dragons.

It was cool here. The girls knelt by small, round pools filled with lukewarm water. It looked like someone had taken a huge watermelon baller, scooped holes in the bottom of the cactus, and filled them with clear water.

The girls scrubbed off dried sand, revealing scratches, cuts, and bruises. Their bodies ached.

Maisy looked at Katy. "I've never seen you so filthy."

Katy looked down at her torn and dirty clothes. Somehow, wearing top brands and fancy clothes didn't seem to matter so much anymore.

No one said anything. They each felt defeated, heartbroken, angry, and scared.

Finally, Katy looked up. "I wonder if people felt like this during World War II. Like the world is ending."

"We have to go home," said Maisy. "We can't do anything to stop Bluebell. It's over."

Lillian didn't look up. She just kept washing her face. Finally, she put her hands on her knees. As the water settled, she saw her reflection. She looked so different. Her hair was shorter, her skin darker, and her eyes wider and with a shade of desperation she had never seen before. Then, as a drop of water fell off her chin, her refection rippled away.

Jack entered the room. "The dragons have summoned you to a meeting," he said.

The girls stood in the main chamber, surrounded by Nevara and three other dragons. Theron represented the griffins and Fred represented the chimeras.

"We've called you here to explain a few things to you," said Nevara. "Then we hope you can clear up a few things for us."

Lillian nodded.

"We lost," continued Nevara, "because we were outnumbered ten to one. We didn't realize how many monsters had been convinced to join their army."

"We now know," said Theron, "that we cannot win by force."

"Jack told us," said Nevara, "that Bluebell has a glowing stone."

Lillian nodded again. She almost felt as if she was on trial. "When I held it, I saw all these visions. Monsters living on earth. The first war. It was as if everything was happening to me."

"Did you know about the stone before you came to Lanodeka?"

Lillian shook her head. "I saw Bluebell with it before she left. But I didn't know it was magical."

"It's more than magical," said Nevara. "The stone is a fragment from the birth of the universe. It's filled with the energy of creation itself. When the monsters were driven out of the human world, we used the stone to create Lanodeka. That's when we realized the stone had more power than we thought. Some wanted to use the stone against the humans and take back the earth. But the dragons and griffins had had enough of violence and war. We had a new world, without humans. We could all be happy here. The other monsters didn't agree.

"We dragons hid the stone where no one could find it. To make sure it was safe, we used a curse to bond the stone to the Stone Keepers, a trusted family who passed it down and kept it secret, generation after generation. Even if someone found the stone, only a Stone Keeper could actually use it.

"Those who wanted the earth back started calling themselves the Earth Keepers. For thousands of years they searched for the Stone Keepers. And finally, they found them."

"Who were they?" asked Lillian.

Nevara raised her eyebrows. "I think you know."

"My mom," said Lillian. *I should be surprised,* she thought, *but somehow, I feel like I've known all along.*

Katy and Maisy looked at each other with wide eyes.

"You're a monster?" asked Maisy.

Before Lillian could answer, Nevara continued. "The monsters could have stolen the stone, but they couldn't use it. They needed someone from your family. We think that's when they started mentoring your sister."

"I saw Bluebell talking to a mermaid when we were little," said Lillian. "She said I just imagined it."

Nevara nodded. "We assume your mom told Bluebell about your family's legacy as Stone Keepers. She was just passing it down, the way her mom had passed it down to her. She had no way of knowing that her daughter was under someone else's influence. Now Bluebell has the stone, and we think we know how the Earth Keepers are going to use it."

"How?" asked Lillian, afraid of the answer.

To everyones surprise, Passiflora stepped into the chamber. "I can answer that," said the dryad.

"Passiflora?" said Katy.

"You remember me." The dryad sounded pleased.

Theron invited her to speak. "Please tell them what you told us."

"When I was a slave for the elves," she began, "I overheard them talking about the Earth Keepers. I asked questions to discover more. The elves couldn't help themselves. They talked about their plans to take the world back. They said that the Earth Keepers had found the stone. I pretended not to believe them. They got mad and said not only did they find the stone, but they also found the Stone Keepers. I mocked them, saying that even if they were telling the truth, the Stone Keepers wouldn't help them. The elves got even more angry and said they already had one Stone Keeper on their side."

The dryad looked sadly at Lillian.

"My sister," said Lillian.

"We had no idea they had the stone," said Nevara.

"Actually," said Theron politely, "we suspected but did not have any proof."

"Even if we had proof," said Nevara, "we never thought that a Stone Keeper would join them."

"What is Bluebell planning to do with the stone?" asked Lillian.

Nevara nodded at Passiflora, who continued.

"That's the worst part. The Earth Keepers are using the stone to create new monsters. They're combining all of our powers into these new creatures. Imagine one monster who could fly, tunnel underground, live underwater, breath fire and ice, turn living things to stone, and control the trees. Now imagine a dozen of these monsters. A hundred. A thousand."

"They would destroy the earth," said Theron.

"But humans have more advanced weapons and technology," said Lillian. "It'll be just like the first war."

Passiflora shook her head. "These new monsters will be different. Some will be hundreds of feet tall. They're unlike anything humans have ever seen."

"But humans have guns, tanks, jets, missiles, and bombs," said Lillian. "Even with a thousand of these mega monsters the Earth Keepers will lose, and millions of people and creatures will die."

"Using the stone," said Passiflora, "the Earth Keepers can open holes to anywhere on earth. Imagine these new monsters climbing out of the ground in any city. In every city. What then? Will humans choose to bomb their own cities?"

"We've done it before," said Maisy.

"Yes," said Theron. "You have a violent history."

"That's not fair," said Katy timidly. "We've done great things too."

"What are your biggest cities?" Passiflora asked.

"New York," said Katy. "Tokyo. Shanghai."

"London," added Lillian. "Moscow. Sydney."

"If monsters appeared in all of those cities," said Passiflora, "would humans bomb them all?"

Lillian shook her head. "That would mean the end of the world."

"That's why the monsters will win," said Nevara, "if we don't stop them."

"If everything you say is true," said Lillian, eyes shining with tears, "then it's impossible. How can you hope to stop them?"

"Actually," said Nevara, "that's where you come in."

"What?" said Lillian.

"We need the stone to win," said Theron.

Lillian held up her hands. "I don't have it."

"But you can get it," said Nevara. "Join Bluebell. Convince her you're on her side. Then take the stone."

"I don't like that idea," said Jack. "It's too dangerous."

"It's too stupid," said Maisy. "Bluebell will never believe it."

"It's too much to ask of one person," said Katy.

"I agree," said Nevara, looking right at Katy.

"Stop right there," said Maisy.

"We're not expecting you to make a decision now," said Nevara, turning back to Lillian. "Go home. Talk to your mother. We'll try to think of other solutions while you're gone. But we don't have much time."

Lillian looked at Theron. "Anything else?"

The griffin shook his head. "I wish there was. But I fear we are running out of options. I am sorry to burden you with this, but I believe the fate of both worlds is in your hands."

Lillian couldn't breathe. She felt as if she had been turned to stone.

"No pressure," said Maisy.

Lillian rested her head on Theron's soft feathers, watching the world slide by thousands of feet below. The wind moved through her hair like a caress, as if this magical world, this monster realm, was trying to comfort her. She felt like she could close her eyes and fall asleep, but didn't want to miss even a moment of the beauty passing below.

Jack and Nevara led the way. Not far behind Lillian, Katy and Maisy rode on a large, black dragon.

Lillian watched as the day over the desert met the night over the mountains. As they flew up toward the snowy peaks, everything grew colder and darker. They were so high, Lillian felt like she could touch the full moon. She reached out a hand to scoop up the stars but they slipped through her fingers. Up ahead, she saw the night over the mountains meet the day over the foothills, like a wall between dark and light, and in a moment, she was under the warm sun again.

Theron glided down toward the foothills. Lillian watched as the rolling land, covered with colorful flowers, turned into a sea of emerald green leaves that rippled as they flew over the forest.

Lillian heard rushing water. She turned her head and saw the majestic waterfall tumbling out of a bank of clouds. She tried to see its source but there wasn't one. It was just there.

Theron turned and flew over the sapphire ocean. Lillian saw the Kraken's dark tentacles flowing underwater. Farther out she saw the sirens swimming, leaving little white crests.

Then she saw the beach, the cliff, and the tunnel. The dragons and griffin flew down and landed in the sand.

Jack, Katy, and Maisy slid off and waited for Lillian, who pressed her face into Theron's neck, hoping the warm feathers would dry her tears. She didn't want anyone to see that she'd been crying the whole way. She climbed off Theron and bowed to the griffin, who bowed in return.

They all said good-bye, then Jack led the girls into the tunnel.

No one said anything as they walked through the tunnel and across the lava path. Jack used his medallion to summon the stone elevator and lower the jetty, and they walked up into the human world.

It was night and the beach was empty. They stood on the sand, looking at each other. No one wanted to say good-bye.

"Any advice?" Lillian asked.

"I don't know what to do, either. But if you need me," Jack said as he placed his medallion around Lillian's neck, "you know where to find me."

Lillian cupped the medallion in her hands. She gazed at the strange runes, the beautiful flowers, and the fierce bird. "Wow," she breathed. "But how will you get back?"

As usual, Jack didn't answer. He just grinned.

Lillian smiled and hugged him. "Thanks for saving our lives." She took a step back so Maisy and Katy could say good-bye.

"I know you don't like hugs," Jack said to Maisy. "So I'll just say good-bye, farewell, see you later, bon voyage, cheers."

Maisy grinned and slugged him on the arm.

Katy threw her arms around Jack. He hugged her tight and whispered, "Take care of Lillian and Maisy."

"I always do," Katy whispered back as tears filled her eyes. "I always will."

Then Jack turned, walked down the jetty and, with a last wave, disappeared into the sea, back to the monster realm.

Epilogue: Home

The girls walked down sleepy streets. The town they knew so well seemed different now, and smaller. More than ever, Lillian adored and appreciated her home.

As they passed the bank, the clock outside read:

2:15 A.M.
Saturday 3-30

"We've been gone five days," said Katy.

Maisy yawned. "Feels like five years."

Katy felt a stab of guilt. "Our poor parents. They'll be so happy to see us."

"Yeah," said Maisy. "Back from the dead."

"How are we going to explain all this?"

"Can we worry about that tomorrow?" asked Lillian. "My head feels like it's about to burst. I can't deal with one more thing right now."

Katy put her arm around Lillian's shoulder.

"That's easy for you to say," said Maisy. "Your mom is a siren."

"Maisy," said Katy.

"What?" said Maisy. "I'm just saying."

Soon they reached Lillian's street. All the houses had their porch lights on, including Lillian's. She felt like that little light was left on just for her.

They stopped on the sidewalk.

"What're you going to do?" asked Maisy.

"You mean, what are *we* going to do?" said Katy.

"I don't know," said Lillian. "I need to talk to my mom."

"The siren," muttered Maisy.

Katy shot her a look.

"I'm just saying," said Maisy.

Lillian smiled. "I wouldn't have made it without you two. So we'll decide together. The three of us."

She hugged Katy. "I love you."

"I love you too," said Katy.

They both looked at Maisy. "And we love you," they said in unison.

Maisy took a step back, out of reach of any hugs. "I love you idiots too."

Then Katy and Maisy turned and walked up the street. Lillian watched them go with a sad smile.

"Five days," said Maisy. "My parents are going to be so mad. I wish *my* mom was a siren."

"Mine are going to cry when they see me," said Katy. "They probably thought I was kidnapped."

"Or dead."

"I don't know how I'm going to explain where we've been and what we've been doing."

"Just say we've been saving the world," said Maisy. "We battled monsters, sailed across dangerous seas, wandered through elf-infested forests, lurked in griffin tunnels, flew dragons, rode chimeras into battle ..." Maisy waved her arms as she acted out their adventures.

Lillian watched as her friends walked away, in and out of the glow of the street lamps, their voices growing fainter and fainter, until they had completely disappeared into the shadows.

Then Lillian turned and walked up to her house. She stood alone on the porch, looking up at the gibbous moon. She was so happy to be back, but she had a feeling she wouldn't be home for long.

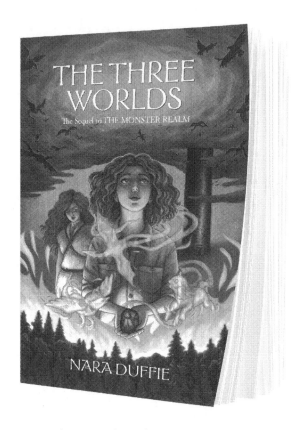

Find out what happens next!

The story continues in the exciting
sequel, *The Three Worlds*.

Learn more at NaraDuffie.com

Afterword & Thanks

About Me and My Novel

When I was seven, I tried writing a novel two or three times. I only wrote a few chapters. Then I got the idea for this book, wrote the first chapter, and stopped again. When was I was nine, my dad told me about National Novel Writing Month. I got excited and signed up.

In September of 2012, my dad taught me how to outline my novel so I'd be ready to write in November when NaNoWriMo started. I wrote 1,000 words a day for the entire month. It was hard, especially because I was learning to type at the same time, but I did it. On November 30th I had my first draft.

And it was terrible! I'm not kidding.

But I wasn't discouraged. In fact, my family and I celebrated. I had a first draft!

Later, when I went back to work on my second draft, I started by reading the book, chapter by chapter. I felt that my first draft was silly and didn't really make much sense. So I hit Command A on the keyboard (Select All) and pressed Delete. Then I started again, and it was much better. My second draft took about six months.

My third draft was also my fourth and maybe fifth draft because I rewrote so many chapters over and over. I wanted my book to be as good as I could write it. In my opinion, rewriting is the hardest part.

My dad acted as my mentor. When I got stuck,

he'd ask me a lot of questions and brainstorm with me to help me understand the scene. Or we'd act it out and then I'd write what happened.

When I was done with my last draft, it turned out that it wasn't my last draft. The story had taken on a life of its own, and the ending was different than I had planned. I had to go back and fix parts of the beginning and middle sections to fit the new ending.

It took about a year and a half to finish my novel. I started when I was nine and finished when I was ten, eleven days before my eleventh birthday.

This is only the first part of a long story. I hope to write more soon.

For Kids Who Want to Write a Novel

While working on my novel I took a pottery class. Later, my dad and I found that working on a potter's wheel was a lot like writing.

First, I centered a lump of clay on my wheel. That was like getting all my ideas down in a first draft, which wasn't much more than a lump of clay. Then as I kept the wheel spinning, I shaped the lump into a vase. That was like writing the second draft of a chapter. Sometimes when you're shaping clay, it falls apart on the wheel. It's OK if you have to start over sometimes. When I was done shaping, it was time to glaze and add any finishing touches. That was like my last draft.

If you think of it that way, writing a novel isn't so overwhelming. If I can do it, you can do it.

Here are ten other things I learned:

- Participate in National Novel Writing Month. The word counter helped me stay motivated, and I had fun meeting other writers at nearby write-ins.
- Stay positive. Don't get discouraged. Even if your first draft is terrible, like mine was, keep going.
- Get a good thesaurus. I recommend the *Oxford American Writer's Thesaurus.* It helped me a lot.
- Take breaks, but not so many that you don't finish.
- Get a mentor and lots of support.
- See it, feel it, write it. This was one of our mottos. It makes writing a little easier.
- Reaction, reaction, reaction. This was another one of our mottos. When anything happens, your characters need to react in their own way.
- Practice instant writing. If you get stuck, just write. Don't let your fingers stop moving. Write whatever comes to mind. Sooner or later, you'll find what you need.
- Enjoy your characters. Whenever I felt tired, Maisy would cheer me up.
- Know when to stop. Your novel doesn't have to be perfect. If you keep trying to make it perfect, you'll edit forever.

Acknowledgements

Thanks to Ed (edwardsweet.com) and Kelly (www.thewriteproofreader.com) for proofreading my book.

Thanks to Elisabeth Alba, one of the best illustrators I've ever seen. She did an amazing job on the book cover, map, and chapter illustrations. You can see more of her work at www.albaillustration.com.

Thanks to Michael Negrete (michaelnegrete.com) for taking my author photo in "the secret forest."

Thanks to National Novel Writing Month for all the encouragement while I was writing (and for introducing me to Klatch Coffee).

Thanks to Collin, one of my best friends, who has been encouraging me ever since I met him. He's fun to hang out with and the only one who saw my map before I finished my novel.

Thanks to my grandma, Sharon Peterson, for supporting me at the L.A. Times Festival of Books.

Thanks to my mom, who is my biggest cheerleader. Whenever I finished a chapter, she was the first one I told. She'd always jump out of her chair and give me a big hug.

Thanks to Hanako, my sister. To give me time to work on my book, she did all of my chores for months and months. She was always positive and never complained. I literally couldn't have finished without her help.

Thanks to my dad who was my editor. He helped me improve my writing and keep my butt in the chair.

When I told my dad I wanted to write a novel that wasn't "kiddy," he took me seriously.

And thanks to Ray Harryhausen. I have been inspired by him since I was seven, when I first saw *Clash of the Titans.* Unlike many of the computerized monsters you see today, Ray's creatures have a lot of personality. You feel for them. His monsters seemed more like a dream, so they weren't too scary. If I hadn't seen Ray's movies, I might not have been inspired to write this story. Ray died on May 7, 2013. I wish I could have met him and given him a copy of my book.

You can contact Nara through her publisher:
share@roamandramble.com

MEDUSA'S
GUITE TO NOVEL WRITING

Are you creative?

Nara's live presentation encourages kids to use their
natural creativity to make something of their own.
Learn more at NaraDuffie.com

Made in the USA
San Bernardino, CA
16 March 2016